You Should be My Baby 2

Kat Washington

D1714913

You Should be My Baby 2

Copyright © 2017 by Kat Washington

Published by Mz. Lady P Presents

www.mzladypresents.com

Table of Contents

Chapter One: Royal

I woke up from sleep that I never meant to have and stretched. Last night, I called Roxy back over here after I left the hospital, because I needed some pussy, and I knew for a fact that she would come back with no hesitation. I decided that, after that, I would stop fucking with her. Every minute I was away from Kaya was making me miss her more and more. I was going to call her today, so that we could talk everything out and hopefully move on from this shit. I just needed to get Roxy out of my house first.

Turning over, I was about to shake Roxy to wake her up, but once I laid my eyes on her, I quickly jumped out of bed. Her throat was slit open, and there was blood everywhere. It was obvious that this had to happen while she was sleeping, because I didn't feel or hear a thing. Who could've done this shit? If they wanted to, they could've easily killed my ass too. The thought of someone being able to break into my house so easily was starting to piss me off.

Looking around the room, there was something that caught my eye. On the wall, big as day, there was writing that read:

KAYA WAS HERE

It was bothering me that she wrote that on the wall with Roxy's blood. How the hell did she get into my house? How is she just gonna kill a girl like this and act like it wasn't a big deal? I needed answers, and I needed them now. I picked up the phone so that I could call her. I wasn't afraid of anything, but Kaya had me feeling some type of way right now. I needed to work on not being such a heavy sleeper. It was going to be the death of me… literally.

"Oh, so now you know how to pick up the phone and call your girlfriend, huh?" Kaya said after letting the phone ring only one time.

"Kaya, what the fuck is wrong with you?!" she just started laughing like I had told the funniest joke, and the shit was pissing me off.

"I see you saw the present that I left for you. Did you like it?" I could hear it in her voice that she was smiling. That's when I realized that this girl was really crazy.

"Are you out of your fucking mind? Why would you do some shit like this?" I asked sitting back down on the bed. I had seen plenty of dead bodies in my life, so seeing Roxy's wasn't really bothering me.

"No nigga, but you were out of yours. You've been ignoring me for how long now? I couldn't even get a text message or anything! Instead of being a man about your shit and telling me how you really feel, you would rather ignore me like a little bitch, then have the nerve to fuck another bitch while we're still in a relationship! Have fun cleaning that shit up, my nigga. Don't call me anymore." and with that being said, she hung up right in my face. I couldn't be mad at anyone but myself, because she was right as hell. I could've called her and told her how I was feeling, but I didn't. In her mind, we were still in a relationship. I didn't even think of that shit. I was only thinking of myself, and now I got to get rid of this damn body.

Picking up my phone again, I called my boy Bo so that he could come with the cleanup crew. Shit like this has never happened to me before, so I didn't know how to feel about it. I wanted to be mad at Kaya, but at the same time, it felt good knowing that her heart was actually in it. She wasn't just in this relationship because of who I was. I fucked all of that up, though. She was done with my ass, and there was nothing that I could do about it.

I thought about going to talk to Kevin and letting him know what his sister had done, but what goes on in our relationship wasn't any of his business. I'd just go to the hospital and see Rome. I knew that he was probably going crazy right now with his own problems, but I needed to talk to someone about this. Shit, he'd cheated on his girl before, and she took his ass right back, so I needed to figure out what the hell he did to get back in good with her, even though she barely trusts his ass now.

I wanted, no, I needed to get Kaya back. She was the only girl that had me in my feelings like this, and I've never cared about anyone's feelings but my own. Now that I know that I hurt Kaya, it's really fucking with me, and I needed to get my shit together ASAP.

The niggas from the cleanup crew came and removed Roxy's body from my crib. It didn't take as long as I thought it would, and I was glad about that. The sooner they got rid of the body, the sooner these niggas could get the fuck up out my shit.

"Damn, nigga. What this bitch do for you to slit her throat like that? She must've been on some grimy shit, huh?" Bo asked laughing. I didn't find any of this funny, so I just stared at him with an emotionless face.

"Do I be in your business, nigga?" I asked.

"Nah man, I was just wondering—" I cut him off before he could continue talking.

"Okay then; don't be all up in my shit then. I pay y'all niggas to clean up, not to be in my business. Hurry up, too. I got shit to do, and y'all niggas are holding me up." Bo didn't say anything else. He did what he had to do, then they all finally left. I wasn't usually this rude to him, but my mood was fucked up right now, and I didn't know how to handle it.

I decided to take a quick shower so that I could go meet Rome down at the hospital. The whole time, the only thing that I could think about was Kaya. I was wondering what she was doing. Was she somewhere crying because of me? Was she with another nigga? The thought of her being laid up with another nigga had me ready to just go find her ass and beg for forgiveness. I knew I wasn't about to do that though. I wasn't a begging ass nigga, and I wasn't about to start being one now.

When I got to the hospital, Clay was lying in bed sleeping, and Rome was sitting in the chair beside her bed looking like he had the weight of the world on his shoulders. I was pretty sure that he felt like shit about what happened to Clay, but he didn't know that crazy bitch was going to just show up and do some shit like this. He looked stressed as hell.

"What's good, nigga?" I asked walking into the room. He looked up at me and gave me a small head nod. He didn't talk much when he had a lot on his mind. He was probably thinking of ways that he could kill that Nikki bitch for fucking with Clay. I didn't blame him, though. If I were him, I'd be on the same shit.

"Has she woken up since yesterday?" I asked.

"Yeah, she woke up. She's not really fucking with me though. She keeps saying that all of this shit is my fault." he said shaking his head.

"You didn't know this shit was going to happen. It's not your fault that the bitch just showed up at your crib."

"It is my fault. None of this shit would've ever happened if I wouldn't have cheated. I'll be lucky if Clay even wants to fuck with me anymore after this."

"I don't think she's going to give up on you like that. You just have to give her some time." He didn't say anything back, so I took that as an advantage to tell him what happened to me since last night. "Kaya broke into my house and killed Roxy." Rome's head shot up quick as hell and looked at me.

"Nigga, what?"

"I was fucking with Roxy just because it was something to do, and I was going to kick her ass out this morning and go patch things up with Kaya. When I woke up this morning, Roxy was dead, and Kaya wrote on the wall that she had done it."

"How the hell did she even get in your house? Damn, she could've killed your ass too if she really wanted to." he let me know.

"I don't know how the hell she got in there. I'm glad she didn't kill my ass, though. Now she wants nothing to do with me, man. This shit crazy."

"Damn, nigga. She's crazy as hell." That's what I need in my life, though. I needed a crazy chick who's not going to let me run all over her and do what I want.

"What should I do to get her back, though?" he shrugged his shoulders.

"Nigga, how am I supposed to know? It took me forever to get Clay back after I cheated." This nigga was no help at all. I sat down in the chair and pulled out my phone. I was seeing if I had any missed calls or anything from Kaya, but I didn't. She probably had my number blocked by now.

"I'm about to get something to eat. You coming?" Rome asked standing up.

"Nah, I'm gonna chill here for a minute." He nodded his head and walked out of the room. I only wanted to stay, because I was hoping that Kaya would come here to check on her friend. I let out a frustrated sigh as I went through my contacts so that I could try to call Kaya.

"You ain't shit, nigga." I heard Clay say. I looked up at her, and she was staring at me like she was disgusted with a nigga or something.

"What you talking 'bout, girl?"

"You know what you did to my best friend. She was head over heels for your stupid ass, and you do her like this? I don't blame her at all for leaving you." I was confused. How the hell did she know what I had done to Kaya already?

"How do you know what happened?" I asked.

"I wasn't sleep. I've been laying here with my eyes closed, because I don't feel like talking to Rome or hearing him apologize some more. That shit is annoying as hell." she said with an eye roll.

"Damn." was all I said. I didn't have anything else to say.

"As for Kaya, you need to give her space right now. She's never been through anything like this before, and she probably doesn't know how to handle it. Having a boyfriend is not something she's used to. Then, on top of that, she had real feelings for your ass, and you did this fuck shit. She just needs to get herself together right now. You constantly calling her isn't going to make her want to talk to you."

I took in everything that she was telling me, but that didn't mean that I was going to listen to her, though. I wasn't about to give Kaya her space. Why would I do that? So she can go

7

out and try to find another nigga? Hell no. That shit wasn't about to happen. Kaya was going to talk to me whether she wanted to or not.

Chapter Two: Kaya

I knew I should've just stayed my ass away from Royal's ass. I should've never got my feelings involved either. This is the exact reason why I stayed away from relationships. Maybe it's just me, but I thought that, in a relationship, there were only supposed to be two people. Or, when there was a problem, you were supposed to talk it out with your significant other. Not ignore them like a fucking child. Now I'm sitting here with my feelings hurt because I decided to give relationships a try. Silly of me.

I didn't like this feeling at all. I'm usually the one that does the heartbreaking. It's never the other way around. I felt so stupid right now. I felt like my heart had been ripped out of my chest. I couldn't get the image of them two lying together out of my head. This shit was the worst. Royal ain't shit, and I'm mad that I even wasted my time on his stupid ass. My phone started ringing, and I answered it.

"Hello?"

"Girl, what the hell have you done? You got Royal coming in my hospital room looking like he's about to cry and shit." Clay says into the phone. I couldn't help but roll my eyes. I don't care about that nigga right now. I'm mad that she's even calling me to talk about him.

"Fuck him." I spat.

"I know exactly how you feel. That's how I felt about Rome after he cheated on me."

"You don't know how I feel, Clay. I knew I should've just stayed away from his stupid ass. Now here I am looking stupid as hell, because the one nigga that I decided to give a chance wants to have community dick and shit."

"It's going to be okay. I promise."

"So, how are you feeling?" I asked, changing the subject. I didn't want to talk about Royal right now. I didn't even want to think about him, but for some reason, I just couldn't get his stupid ass out of my head.

"I will feel a lot better once I get my hands on that Nikki bitch. She deserves to die, and I'm the one that needs to kill her." I was shocked as hell at her. Clay wasn't really a violent person, but ever since Nikki had been trying her, she's turned into a completely different person.

"I'll be up there later to check on you. I know you're tired of being around Rome and his apologizing." I chuckled. I knew that Rome had probably apologized one hundred times by now.

"Girl, you don't know the half of it, but don't come visit me. I know you're probably feeling like shit right now, and you don't want to be bothered with people. Just stay home today. I'll be good; I promise." she said. She was right. I didn't want to be bothered at all. I didn't even want to leave the house, but I knew if I stayed here that my thoughts would be consumed with Royal and I wasn't trying to do that.

After I got off of the phone with Clay, I decided to go downstairs and get me something to drink. I don't even care that it's still early in the day. I just wanted to be drunk and maybe I could go to sleep for the rest of the day.

"What you doing?" I heard Kevin ask as I poured me some Ciroc. I didn't even hear him come into the house. I turned around to look at him and he had Reese standing right beside him. She seemed like she was a really sweet girl. She and I could probably hang out sometimes.

"I'm drinking. What does it look like?" I asked sitting down at the kitchen table.

"Damn, it's not even one o'clock yet, and you're already drinking? What the hell done happened to you?" I rolled my eyes, shocked at the fact that Royal hasn't told Kevin about what I did. Looking back at the whole situation, I should've done more damage. I should've fucked his house up before I left. Turned on all of the water and made that bitch flood or something. I already know that I couldn't have killed him, even though his ass deserved it. My feelings for him were way too strong, and I would hate to see him hurt. Isn't that some shit? That nigga ripped my heart out, and I'm over here saying I would hate to see him hurt. This nigga got me turning into a completely different person.

"You don't hear me talking to you?" Kevin asked.

"Nope. I wasn't listening." I noticed that Reese was no longer standing beside him, so she was probably upstairs already.

"What's going on with you?"

"Nothing." I quickly lied. He gave me a knowing look.

"So you look like you just lost your best friend and you're drinking early as hell for no reason? Man, tell me what's wrong with you." I knew that he wasn't going to let this go until I told him what was wrong with me. He's always been like this. He won't let me just be in my feelings. He always wants me to talk about it and shit. He's always telling me how keeping my feelings all bottled up like I do isn't healthy. Blah, blah, blah. That's what I do. I like to keep shit to myself. Plus, I didn't like people all up in my business.

I sighed and downed my drink before I started talking. I told him everything that happened starting from Royal ignoring me and me walking into his house and finding him in the bed with another bitch. Let's not forget that the bitch was naked too. He looked shocked after I told him the story, but I knew he wasn't shocked about me killing Roxy. He knew killing wasn't shit for me.

"Damn, you must really like this nigga if you're killing bitches over him and shit." he said.

"I mean…We were in a relationship. You don't do something like that when you're in a relationship. That's just how it goes. If he wanted to fuck with other bitches, then his stupid ass should've stayed single." I said shaking my head. That's when I felt my eyes burning. *Man, hell nah.* I thought to myself. I know I'm not sitting here about to cry over this nigga. I started blinking rapidly, and Kevin just stared at me.

"Well, I guess you could say that y'all are even right?" he asked.

"What? What are you talking about?"

"You robbed him, and he cheated on you. Y'all are even." I couldn't believe this nigga had really just said this shit to me. I just looked at him with my mouth hanging open and everything. I thought about hitting his ass, or even throwing my drink in his face, but Kevin was just as crazy as I was. We would be fighting up in this bitch, and I really didn't need that right now.

"Why the fuck didn't you tell me he lived at that house?" I asked trying my hardest to remain calm.

"You had no business trying to hit a lick without me anyway. That's what you get." I didn't have anything else to say to him. I really just wanted to hit him right now, but what good would that do? Yeah, it would make me feel better, but not for long.

Now that I think about it, I didn't even feel bad about robbing his ass. *Fuck him.* I thought to myself. Maybe if I keep saying it, then I will actually start to feel like that. I sure hope so, because I don't like feeling like this. Being sad is not what's up.

"I'm taking my ass upstairs since you in your own little world over there and shit. It'll all work itself out. It always does." Kevin said standing up from the table and making his way upstairs. I got up and poured me another drink. I planned to be drunk within the next ten minutes, because I didn't want to think about any of this anymore. My phone rang again, and it was Mecca calling. What the hell did this nigga want? Rolling my eyes, I answered the phone.

"Hello?"

"So you just forgot about my ass, huh?" he asked sounding like a little bitch.

"Well, I'm trying to, but I can't do that with you calling me and shit."

"Damn, all I did was ask a question. I heard you were in a relationship now." This nigga really just called me just to talk about the relationship that I'm no longer in? What kind of shit was he on?

"Why is that any of your business what I do?" I snapped.

"I was just wondering why you could never give me a chance, but you were quick to hop on the next nigga's dick. He must got hella money." Oh, the disrespect that I was receiving right now. He was really in his little feelings.

"Yep, I was. You wanna know why? His money is longer than yours, by far, his dick is way bigger than yours, and you wanna know the best part? He's not a pussy. I could ask that nigga to go rob someone with me, and he would tell my ass to stay home because he's got it. You on the other hand was about to piss on yourself when I asked you to do it. I needed a real nigga, Mecca. Not a pussy."

"Bitch…" was all that he was able to get out before I hung up on him. Why the hell did he call my phone on some bitch shit like that? If I wanted Mecca, then I damn sure would've been with him. He is really mad, because I didn't want to be with him. He tried it. I shook my head as I started drinking from the Ciroc bottle. Fuck pouring me glasses. That shit wasn't working like I wanted it to.

Once I was good and drunk, I staggered up the stairs so that I could go to my room. I heard moaning coming from Kevin's room, and I threw up a little bit in my mouth. Tomorrow, I was definitely going to look for my own place. This shit wasn't going to work anymore.

I finally made it to my bed and fell face first on it. I didn't even have the strength to fix myself so that I was comfortable. I just passed out in that position.

***

I woke up with a banging headache, and I was laying on something hard as hell. Damn, I shouldn't have got drunk like that because I was now regretting it. I probably won't even go to work tonight. I sat up in bed and stretched. The only thing was, I wasn't in bed. I was on the floor. *When the hell did I get on the floor?* Looking around, I noticed that I was on Royal's lap. He was sleeping with his back against the wall. When the hell did he get here? No, why the hell was he even here? How did he even get in my room? Why am I on his lap? There were so many unanswered questions, and it was pissing me off.

Looking at his fine ass sleep made me mad as hell. Now, he wanted to be all up under me after he had got caught with another bitch? It hasn't even been a full day yet, and here he is all up in my personal space. Without thinking, I balled my fist up and punched him hard as hell in his jaw. He instantly woke up.

"Man, what the fuck?!" he yelled holding his jaw.

"Get the fuck out! Why are you even here?!" I yelled.

"Because I wanted to talk. We didn't do much talking though." he said with a smirk on his face. That's when I noticed that I was naked as the day I was born and so was he. I couldn't remember anything. I quickly got up and found some shorts and a tank top to put on. I felt so disgusting right now.

"Leave." I said pointing towards the door.

"Not until you talk to me." he said standing to his feet, dick swinging and all. I bit my lip and had to look away. With the way that he was looking, there wasn't going to be any talking. That's probably what happened the first time. He came in here looking all good and my drunk ass just jumped on him. I was so ashamed of myself.

"There's nothing to talk about, nigga! You still want to stick your dick in other bitches. Go be single! You can do whatever you want, then."

"The only bitch I want to stick my dick in is you!" I folded my arms across my chest.

"Lying ass, nigga. If that was the case, then I wouldn't have found you in bed with Roxy. Will you please just get out? We have nothing to talk about. You showed me who it was that you wanted. I would tell you to go be with her, but we both know why that can't happen." he pushed his dreads out of his face and let out a frustrated sigh. Damn, why did he have to act up? He could've been daddy.

"I'll be back tomorrow or some shit." he said, as he put his clothes back on. I didn't say anything back to him. I guess I was going to have to find somewhere else to go tomorrow, because I really didn't want to see his stupid ass face tomorrow. Or ever for that matter. He looked at me one last time before he left out of the room. I don't know why, but for some reason, I felt sad as hell watching him leave. I sat down on the bed and shook my head. This was too much for me. I'll be glad when I get over his ass completely. I just wanted to move on with my life, but I couldn't do that with him popping up and shit. Something had to give, and soon.

Chapter Three: Clay

I was beyond ready to go home and get the hell out of this hospital bed. It was uncomfortable and I was ready to be back in my bed so that I could finish this healing process. Once I was done healing, I was going to go look for the Nikki bitch. She better be glad that my baby made it. If she would've killed my child, then I probably would've killed her whole family and made her suffer through that hurt and pain.

"Have you ate anything today? You need to feed my son." Rome said coming into the room with a bag from McDonalds. He swore up and down that we were having a boy. I wanted a little girl though.

"I'm not hungry." I lied. I was hungry as hell, but I didn't want anything to do with Rome right now. I didn't even want the food that he kept trying to force me to eat. I was mad at him. This was all his fault and I didn't care what anyone said. If he would've never cheated, then I wouldn't have gotten attacked. I was glad that Erica was there to save my ass because who knows what would've happened if she wasn't. My ass would probably be dead right now.

"I don't care about none of that shit. You can be mad at me all you want, but you're not about to sit here and starve my child like you've lost your damn mind." he said sitting down in the chair that was beside my bed. I didn't say anything to him. I just snatched the bag out of his hand and pulled out the burger that was in there. Rome watched me the whole time as I ate the burger like I hadn't eaten anything in years.

"You can stop staring at me now." I said.

"How long are you going to be mad at me?"

"Forever." I knew damn well I wasn't going to be mad at him forever, because I could never stay mad at him for too long. I wasn't very good at holding grudges.

"How many times do I have to apologize to you? You can't be mad at me. I didn't know that she was going to show up to the house and do this fuck shit." he said. I could tell that this whole situation was stressing him out, but I didn't care at all. How he think I felt?

"But if it wasn't for you fucking that bitch in the house that we shared, none of this would've happened. She shouldn't have even known where the hell we lived at, Rome. So yeah. I can be mad at you. You brought another bitch in the house that we shared, fucked her, and she tried to kill me all because of you. I'm in this hospital right now because of you." I hope that I was hurting his feelings right now. I was so hurt when I walked in on him cheating on me. I want to be able to trust him again, but it seems like that's never going to happen.

"Oh my poor baby! Who did this to you? I know it was one of his side hoes!" my mom yelled walking into the room.

I didn't even want her here. I told Rome not to call her and he did it anyway. I was not trying to hear her mouth.

"I'm fine, Mom." I said with a sigh.

"You don't look fine to me. I can't believe you let one of your little sluts do this to my child. What the hell is wrong with you? You need to learn to control your bitches, Romeo." my mom said pointing her finger in Rome's face. I could tell that she was pissing him off, but he wasn't going to disrespect her. No matter how rude she was to him, he was still respectful. I admired him for that, because sometimes, my mom needed to get cussed out. She doesn't know when to stop.

"She wasn't one of my hoes. I was at work when all of this happened." Rome said in a calm voice.

"That's bullshit and you know it! You were probably on the way to see another one of your bitches. I don't know what the hell my daughter sees in you. She should've left your ass when she caught you with another bitch in the house you all share."

"Mom, could you not?" I asked. This was getting annoying as hell. I wish that she would just leave. I'll just visit her once I'm healed.

"No, he needs to hear this. He needs to know that what he is doing isn't going to fly with me. Just because my daughter is okay with you cheating on her, doesn't mean that I am. She deserves better." My mom shook her head as she looked at Rome like he was the scum of the earth. He was clenching his jaw, and I knew he was seconds from saying something to my mom that he would regret later.

"I'll be back later." Rome said standing up. He kissed me on my forehead before he walked out of the room.

"And don't come back!" my mom yelled after him. She was making things so much worse.

"You didn't have to do that. He already feels like shit about what happened, and you coming in here yelling isn't making things any better." I said. My mom waved me off and sat down.

"He needed to hear it because I know you wouldn't tell him. You just need to leave him alone, Clay. He's been nothing but trouble since you first got with him. Why are you okay with a man who constantly cheats on you?"

"He's not cheating on me! He cheated on me once and that was it. You need to let that go, because I did. He makes me happy and that's all that matters. Why isn't that good enough for you?" I asked trying not to lose my temper.

"You honestly believe that? You honestly think that he's not cheating on you, Clay? Once a cheater, always a cheater. I thought I taught you that when you were a little younger, but I guess not. There are plenty of men that are better than him, Clay. You don't have to be with him just because he pays your bills."

"I'm not with him just because he pays my bills. I'm with him because I actually love him…" I started but she cut me off.

"You love him? Child please, just because a man cheats on you and you stay, that doesn't mean it's love. That right there, sweetheart; it's called stupidity." I know it sounds bad, but I wanted to strangle my mom right now. She didn't care about my well-being at all. All she was worried about was me leaving Rome, but that wasn't going to happen though.

"Well, I'll be stupid then. I'm carrying his baby, and we're not breaking up no time soon." I let her know.

"You're what?! You need to get rid of it! Why would you want to keep a baby by someone who doesn't love you the way he should?" Before I could cuss her stupid ass out, Kaya walked into the room with a look of disgust on her face. She doesn't like my mom at all and the feeling was mutual.

"Hey Clay, are you feeling better today?" Kaya asked purposely ignoring my mom.

"Yes. I'm feeling a lot better. I'll probably be able to leave tomorrow." I let her know.

"Excuse us, but we were having a conversation before you just barged in here." my mom told Kaya. Kaya scoffed.

"Obviously, the conversation wasn't that important then." She said. My mom ignored her and turned back to me.

"You need to get rid of that baby you're carrying. You're not even married, and Rome is still cheating on you. You want these other women around your child? That's exactly what's going to happen if you stay with him." I didn't even get to respond to my mom, because Kaya spoke up.

"What kind of shit is that to say to your own child? Just because you can't get a man that doesn't beat on you, doesn't mean all men ain't shit. Rome loves Clay and Clay loves Rome. Instead of being a hater like you're doing, you should be happy that your daughter is happy. This is why no one wants to be around you now. You think you're better than everybody, when really, you ain't shit. Go find you some business and stay out of Clay's. She's a grown woman and can make her own decisions." My mom was shocked at what Kaya had said to her. To be honest, I was too. I knew Kaya didn't like her, but damn.

"Excuse me?" was all my mom could say.

"You heard every word I said. Why are you even here? I'm pretty sure Clay didn't call your ass. That should tell you something. Your daughter gets hurt and doesn't even call you." Kaya was making things worse.

"I'm not going anywhere. This is my child and I have every right to be here." my mom said folding her arms across her chest.

"Mom, I think it's best if you leave." I said. She looked at me with wide eyes, but she didn't say anything. She gave Kaya a menacing look before turning to leave out of the room. *Finally.* I thought to myself.

"Why was she even here?" Kaya asked pulling out her ringing phone.

"Rome insisted on calling her. I told him not to, but you know that nigga doesn't listen to my ass. She came in here talking all this shit to him and he had to leave. I know he was ready to cuss her out."

"Shit, I was ready to cuss her out. I really can't stand her. I don't know how you deal with her on a regular basis." Kaya's phone started ringing again but she ignored it.

"Who the hell is blowing you up like that?" I asked.

"Royal's stupid ass. He's been calling and texting me all day. It's starting to piss me off."

"When's the last time you talked to him?"

"Yesterday. I got drunk, and he came over and we had sex." she said putting her head down in shame. I was shocked as hell.

"What? What you mean you had sex with him? You're supposed to be teaching him a lesson, not fucking him!"

"I know! I don't even remember having sex with him. I was drinking by myself, then I went upstairs and just passed out. I woke up naked on the floor in Royal's lap. I don't remember him even coming in the room. I don't remember shit. I told his ass to leave as soon as I got up though. He keeps saying that he wants to talk to me, but I don't have anything to say to him." Her phone started ringing again, so she turned it all the way off.

"Maybe you should just hear him out. I told him to stay away from you for a couple of days but it's obvious that he doesn't listen." I said watching her twist her face up.

"Hear him out? He cheated on me and got caught. That's the end of it." I hated that she had to experience this.

25

No one should have to go through the pain of getting cheated on by the person they love or care about. I wouldn't wish that on my worst enemy.

"It might make you feel better about it though." I said. She rolled her eyes.

"I'm good. There's nothing to feel better about because I'm over him." She was definitely lying, but I was going to let her have it.

"You're over me?" I heard a voice say from the entrance of my room. Looking up, there stood Royal looking directly at Kaya. I didn't expect him to show up again today since he came by yesterday. I knew he only stopped by because he thought Kaya was going to be here. He wasn't fooling nobody.

"Yep." Kaya said without looking at him. He knew she was lying just like I did.

"Let me talk to you real quick." he said. She looked up at him then quickly looked away. She looked as if she wanted to jump in his arms right about now.

"I told you we have nothing to—"

"Kaya, get the fuck up before I drag you out of this damn room. I'm tired of playing with yo' ass man." he said cutting her off. She looked at him like he had lost his mind, but her ass got up out of that chair. She slowly followed behind him. I couldn't do anything but laugh. She was putting on this front, but I knew she wanted that nigga back just as much as he wanted her back. I just hope they can get their shit together without me being in the middle of it.

   ***

"Do you need anything? You good?" Rome asked me as I laid in bed. I was finally home from the hospital and I couldn't have been happier. It felt so good being in my bed and not that stupid ass hospital bed. They only kept me there because they said my blood pressure was high and they wanted to monitor it because it was bad for the baby. I was only about six weeks along in my pregnancy too.

"Yes, I'm good." I said. Rome hasn't really said much to me since my mom came into the hospital room running her damn mouth. At first, I didn't care because I was still a little mad at him, but now it's starting to bother me. It's not my fault that my mom said all of that stupid shit. He had no reason to be mad at me.

"Cool. I'll be back later." he said getting his things together so that he could leave.

"Where are you going? I asked.

"To work and to handle some shit." He didn't even look at me when he said it. His back was to me and everything. I immediately started to feel some type of way.

"It's Sunday, Rome. Your shop is closed. Now where the hell are you going?" I asked sitting up in bed and folding my arms across my chest. That's why he didn't turn around. He knew he was lying and didn't want me to see through it. Too bad he thought of a terrible lie.

27

"I'm going to handle some shit, aight?" he said turning to look at me. That still didn't tell me what I wanted to hear. I was starting to get pissed off. Why the hell was he playing?

"Where the fuck are you going, Romeo?" he sighed and ran his hand down his face.

"I just need some space." he had the nerve to say.

"Space? Space for what nigga? You better take your ass to the next room if you feel like you need some space. What the hell have I done to you to make you feel like you need some space? You're the one that's been avoiding me!"

"See, this is why I didn't want to say shit to your ass. I knew you were going to overreact like you're doing right now. Just chill out. I need space away from you. Nothing more, nothing less." He was acting like what he was saying to me was okay. Who says shit like this to their fiancé?

"So, what? You wanna be single or something?" I asked, not really sure if I really wanted that answer or not.

"I thought about it." I felt my heart sank into the pit of my stomach. Why the hell was he thinking about being single? And why the hell hasn't he told me any of this?

"Why?" I asked trying my hardest to hold back the tears that were threatening to fall.

"You deserve better like your mom said. You could do so much better than me. You don't trust me anyway, so it's not like you'll miss me that much." He shrugged his shoulders.

"Fuck what my mom has to say! If I'm still here, there's obviously a reason behind it. You didn't even talk to me about how you felt. You just started avoiding me." What was up with niggas? Why did they act like they couldn't tell someone how they were feeling? He didn't say anything for a while. He just looked at me.

"I'll be back later." he said and turned to leave. I just sat there in shock. I couldn't believe this nigga had actually just left like that. Shit, since he wanted to be single, I was going to let him. I had no problem being a single mother. The only thing was, I didn't want to be a single mother. I wanted Rome to be there through the whole thing, but I guess we can't always get what we want in life.

Chapter Four: Rome

I wasn't lying when I told Clay that I needed some space. Being around her right now was only making me feel worse about what Nikki did to her. Plus, I felt like everything that her mom said yesterday at the hospital was true. She really did deserve someone better than me. She deserved the world, and it was seeming like I wasn't the nigga that was going to be able to provide that for her.

I felt bad about just leaving while she was trying to figure out what was going on with me, but I really did have shit that I needed to handle. I needed to go to the hospital and talk to Nikki. She hadn't been released yet, and I was happy about that. She needed to know that she fucked up when she showed up at my house and attacked Clay. She just better be glad that Clay didn't lose the baby she's carrying.

I knew that I was going to have to kill Nikki. She took things way too far. I know for a fact if Clay ever sees Nikki again, she's going to have a problem that I didn't do something about her. I was just going to do it now to get it over with before Nikki got better and decided to try to come at Clay again. I wasn't having that. Her crazy ass needed to be dealt with right now.

When I pulled up to the hospital, I quickly got out of the car and walked through the doors. I had no idea what room she was in, but I was sure that it was going to be easy for me to find out. I walked up to the desk where the receptionist was sitting. She was light-skinned with long weave that looked cheap as hell. She had green contacts in and way too much lip gloss. She actually looked like she would be cute if she didn't do all of this extra shit.

"Hey sexy, what can I help you with?" she asked trying her hardest to be cute. It wasn't working though. I only had eyes for Clay anyway.

"I'm looking for a Nikki Reed." I let her know. She started typing on her computer, then she told me what room Nikki was in.

"Is she your girlfriend or something?" she asked before I walked away.

"Nah."

"Oh, well maybe you should take my number and we can hang out sometime." I just chuckled at her.

"Nah, I got a woman at home. Even if I didn't, I couldn't fuck with you because you try to be someone you're not. Take out that ugly weave and those contacts, then you might be able to find someone who will actually give you the time of day." Her mouth fell open, but before she could say anything, I was heading towards Nikki's room. Ole girl needed some new friends. They were wrong as hell for letting her walk out of the house like that.

"I knew you would come and see me." Nikki said when I walked in her room. Her eyes lit up and everything.

"I'm not here to check on you, Nikki. You did some fucked up shit and you must be out of your damn mind if you think I'm going to let that shit slide." I let her know. The smile on her face faded.

"What are you talking about? She attacked me, so I came back and got my revenge. I bet you didn't even get mad at her for beating my ass."

"Don't be mad at me because you can't fight. What you did was uncalled for. Showing up to my house is one thing, but you showed up to my house and put your hands on my fiancé. My fiancé that's currently carrying our baby. Do you see where you were wrong, or no?" Out of nowhere, she started crying. *Man, what the fuck?*

"Why don't you love me like you love her? I'm so much better for you! I bet she can't even fuck you like I can. You know my sex was better." This bitch was really crazy. I knew I should've never even fucked with her to begin with.

"I don't have feelings for you, Nikki. I've been with Clay since high school. What makes you think I'm going to leave her for you? You fucked me knowing I had a girlfriend. You're not wifey material at all." This conversation was pointless. I was never going to be with her. I just wished she could get that through her head. Well, I guess it didn't even matter now, because she was about to die anyway. As I was reaching to pull my gun out, I heard someone walk in the room.

"Hey, Nikki, I brought you some food." some girl said. I turned around and came face to face with a sexy ass, dark-skinned girl.

"Thanks, I'm starving." Nikki said quickly wiping her tears so the girl wouldn't see them.

"Who is this?" she asked pointing to me.

"This is my man, Rome that I've been telling you about." This bitch.

"I'm not her man, and I never will be. I was just on my way out though." I turned to leave out of the hospital room. I was mad as hell right now. Whoever that dark-skinned bitch was fucking me up. I knew I shouldn't have tried talking to Nikki. I should've just gone in there, handled my business, and left before anyone noticed that she was dead. As I was walking, I bumped into someone.

"Excuse me." I said.

"You need to watch where you're going next time." I knew that voice all too well. It was Tracy, Clay's mom. I couldn't stand her ass.

"Yeah." was all I said as I continued to walk out.

"Wait," she said grabbing me by my arm. Why the hell was she even here to begin with? Clay wasn't even in the hospital anymore. "I need to talk to you." I sighed loudly because it wasn't no secret that I didn't like her. What could she possibly want to talk to me about?

"What?" I asked.

"I just wanted to talk to you, since I know that you have no problem cheating on my daughter." I bit the inside of my cheek because I really wanted to strangle this woman.

"Talk about what?"

"Clay doesn't know how to handle a man like you. You need to know what it's like to be with a real woman, like me." I just stared at her like she had lost her mind. She must've lost her mind. Was she serious right now?

"A real woman like you?" I laughed.

"Yes. Just because I'm older doesn't mean I don't know how to suck a dick. I've been wanting to suck yours for a couple of years now, but I can't convince Clay to leave you so that I can do that."

"You're her mom. Why would you want to see her hurt? You know damn well if I told her that you're trying to fuck me, she isn't going to be too happy about that."

"I'll just let her know the reason you were at the hospital today. I'm pretty sure that she doesn't even know that you came to visit the girl that put her in the hospital to begin with. We wouldn't want her to find out, would we?" I couldn't believe that she was trying to blackmail me right now. How did she even know that I was here to see Nikki in the first place? Was this bitch following me?

"Tracy, get the fuck on with that shit." I said walking away again.

"She can't handle you like I can, Romeo!" she called out from behind me. I just shook my head. I couldn't believe this shit. I wanted to tell Clay what her mom had said to me, but I already knew that would start a lot of drama that could be avoided. I just sat in my car and wondered what I should do. I didn't get to handle Nikki like I wanted to and now Clay's mom was trippin'. I didn't know when they were going to release Nikki from the hospital, but I needed to get her before she went home. Or I could just go to her house and murk her ass. That will probably be easier anyway.

Starting my car, I headed in the direction of my mom's house. I hadn't talked to her in a little minute because there was a lot that had been going on. I'm pretty sure she's going to cuss me out for not picking up the phone and calling her, but I was prepared for it. She didn't know about half of the shit that was going on in my life right now. I wasn't the type to tell my mom my business about my relationship, but right now, I just needed some advice.

My mom had been living in the same house in the hood since I was a young nigga. I told her that I would buy her a nice house closer to mine, but she wasn't trying to hear that. She claimed she was perfectly fine living where she was at. I eventually gave up trying to convince her to move. Niggas knew not to fuck with her though.

There was a car that I had never seen before parked behind hers in the driveway. I hoped like hell it wasn't no nigga in there fucking my mom. I wouldn't hesitate to kill his ass, and I really didn't care how my mom felt about it. I guess I could've called first, but I just like to show up.

Getting out the car, I made my way to the front door which was unlocked. Whatever she was cooking smelled good as hell. My mom cooked every night like it was Sunday dinner. I needed to start bringing my ass over here more so I could get some of her good ass cooking. Don't get me wrong, Clay was a beast in the kitchen too, but she wasn't my mom.

"Don't be walking up in my house like you own the place. Especially after you ignore me for a year." my mom said walking up to me.

"Stop playing; it's only been a couple of weeks." I laughed pulling her in for a hug.

"Well, don't let it happen again. Where's Clay at? I feel like I haven't seen her in years." My mom loved Clay. I knew she was going to have a lot to say after I tell her what's going on with us.

"She's at the house probably sleeping or something. That's what I came over here to talk to you about." I said walking into the living room so I could sit on the couch.

"Oh Lord. What you done did to that girl, now?" she asked sitting down next to me.

"Well, she just got out of the hospital because she was attacked…" I started.

"Attacked?! Who was she attacked by?"

"The girl I cheated on her with." I thought my mom was about to hit my ass, and I was shocked when she didn't. She was looking at me like she wanted to hit me though. I didn't blame her at all.

"And she hasn't left you yet?" Yet? The fuck she mean yet?

"Nah, but I kinda told her that I wanted to be single before I left the house. I haven't talked to her since then."

"Why would you say that? Do you really want to be single?"

"Well, when she was in the hospital, her mom came yelling at me and telling me how Clay deserves better and basically I ain't shit and I started to believe her. Clay does deserve better than me. If I would've never cheated, she wouldn't have ended up in the hospital to begin with." I admitted.

"You can't care about how other people feel about your relationship, Rome. As long as you're happy and she's happy, that's all that matters."

"Yeah, but I don't feel like she's happy anymore. She doesn't even trust me."

"Well you can't blame her for that. It's going to take some time for her to trust you again. You just need to make sure that other girl doesn't bother you two anymore."

"Oh, and her mom is trying to have sex with me. I don't know what to do about that." the thought of Clay's mom wanting to have sex with me made me want to throw up. She wasn't an ugly woman at all, but she was old enough to be my mom and she was my girl's mother. Who does some foul shit like that?

"You need to tell Clay!" I knew that was going to be her answer. I wasn't going to do that though. Not until Nikki was dead and gone so Tracy wouldn't have anything to blackmail me with.

"Sounds to me like Clay needs to come fuck with a real nigga." a voice said from behind us. I knew that voice all too well and it pissed me off. I stood up and walked right over to my older brother Raymond. He had a smirk on his face, but it wouldn't be there for long.

"The fuck you say, nigga?" I asked getting in his face. Everyone knew that I could beat his ass. I had already done it that day at the bar when he had his bitch ass hands on Clay. I don't know why he kept trying me. He must like getting his ass beat or something.

"You heard what I said little bro. Clay needs to be with a nigga like me. She could pop out all of my babies and we could live happily ever after and shit." he laughed like this shit was funny. Clay wasn't having anyone's babies unless they were mine. The fuck this nigga think he is?

In the middle of his laughter, I two-pieced his ass and made him fall to the ground. He got up like he was about to do something, but I already had my gun out and aimed at his head. I could see the fear in his eyes, but he was still trying to act tough. Bitch ass nigga.

"Talk all that shit now, pussy." I spat. I heard my mom yelling for me to stop, but it was falling on deaf ears right now. I really wanted to splatter this nigga's brains all over the wall and I wouldn't lose not one ounce of sleep over it either. I couldn't do that to my mom though.

"Pull the trigger, nigga." he said.

"Romeo, put the gun down. He's not worth you going to jail for the rest of your life." my mom said. She was right, but I still wanted to shoot this nigga dead in his shit. I lowered the gun and started walking towards the door.

"Don't think this is over my nigga. Tell your boy Royal that he'll be getting a visit from me real soon." he said as I walked out of the door. What he said made me want to go back in there and actually shoot his ass, but I kept walking to my car. Raymond was a pussy. He wasn't going to do shit, and that was a fact.

When I pulled up in the driveway, I wasn't sure if I actually wanted to go in there or not. I wasn't sure how Clay was feeling about me right now, and I really wasn't in the mood to be arguing with her ass right now. Maybe she would be taking a nap when I got in there. I sure hoped she was.

Getting out of the car, I slowly walked up to the front door and unlocked it. It smelled good as hell in here but I wasn't hungry since I had already eaten at my mom's. She knows she was supposed to be in bed resting, but she had to be hard-headed. She could've easily ordered some food, but she wanted to be up moving and shit. I bet she was going to be complaining later about how sore she is.

Clay was sitting at the kitchen table with a big plate of spaghetti in front of her. She was eating like she hadn't eaten anything in days. I chuckled to myself because I knew it was my son that had her eating like this. I walked over to the table and sat down in front of her. She didn't even look up at me. She just kept eating like I wasn't even there.

"So you gonna ignore me like I'm not sitting here?" I asked after five minutes of just sitting in silence. She finally looked up at me and rolled her eyes.

"Hey." she said dryly. I couldn't help but laugh. I knew she was still feeling some type of way about what I said to her earlier, but I needed her to let that go. I didn't want to be single, and I damn sure didn't want her to be available to another nigga. She was carrying my baby and soon she'll be carrying my last name too.

"We need to talk about what I said earlier." She rolled her eyes again and scoffed.

"About how you want to be single?" she snapped.

"Man, chill. I didn't mean that shit. I just said it out of anger. I shouldn't have said that then left you here by yourself."

"Yeah, you shouldn't have said that. You also shouldn't have lied to me about where you were going. I don't know why you insist on lying to me like I don't know when you're lying. Nigga, I know you better than you know yourself." She finished what was on her plate and got up so that she could get some more. *Fat ass.* I laughed to myself.

"Well, let's forget that even happened." I said watching her devour her plate.

"I bet you do want me to forget about you lying to me. That's not going to happen though. I find out everything, remember?" She smirked at me and it made me nervous as hell. It was like she knew what I had done today. I still wasn't going to let her know though. Not until I got rid of Nikki for good. I didn't know how she was going to react about her mom, but I knew I had to tell her. That was probably going to be the hardest thing I ever had to do though.

"I know you probably want to handle Nikki by yourself, but I need to do it. She's gotten away with way too many things and that's all because of you. I got this." she said finishing up her second plate and getting up to put it in the sink.

"Got me fucked up. You ain't gonna do shit but stay your ass in the house and make sure my son is good. I got this." I should've known that she was going to want to get Nikki herself, but I couldn't let that happen. Clay might get hurt and I wasn't having that.

"See that's the thing. I don't even know if you mean that shit. For all I know, you could pay the bitch and have her relocate or some shit. She should've been dead after we fought at your shop. She shouldn't have even been in there with her hands all over you and shit. Then you went to make sure she was okay before you made sure I was okay. What kind of shit is that? I don't trust you with this situation at all. So like I said, *I* got this." She didn't even let me respond to her before she just left out the kitchen. That shit had me mad as hell.

Getting up from the table, I went to go find her. She wasn't about to do shit but stay her ass in the house. I know I fucked up before when it came to Nikki, but this time I'm serious about getting rid of her. She took shit too far by showing up at my crib. That's another thing I needed to look into. We had to move. With her knowing where we live at, it isn't going to end well. I just had a feeling that she was going to show back up and try to do something to Clay again.

"You got me fucked up, Clay. I know one thing, though. You better stay your hard-headed ass in this mother fucking house or we're going to have some serious problems." I said once I got in our bedroom. She was sitting on the bed flipping through the channels on TV.

"Whatever nigga." she said waving me off. I hated when she got like this. Everything that I was saying to her right now was falling on death ears. She was going to do whatever she wanted, and it wasn't going to do anything but make me mad.

"I'm serious, Clay. Make me put my foot in your ass."

"Nigga, shut the hell up. I'm trying to watch TV, and you're over here talking all loud and shit." I snatched the remote from her and turned the TV off. I needed her to know how serious I was about her not doing shit to Nikki. I had everything under control.

"If I find out you doing shit behind my back, we gonna have some problems, aight?" She looked at me with her arms folded pouting like a big ass kid. I knew she was only mad because I had just turned off the TV, but it got her attention so I was good.

"I hear you, Rome." she said rolling her eyes yet again. Her little attitude wasn't doing shit but making me want to slide up in her real quick. She was wearing some small ass shorts that her ass was hanging out of. I guess she saw me eyeing her body because she started shaking her head.

"Nah nigga, you ain't getting shit so you can stop looking at me like that. I'm too sore to do anything with you anyway." she said.

"Well just lay there while I do everything." I said walking over to the bed and gently tugging at her shorts.

"No. I'm tired and I'm about to take a nap. Use your hand or something." She turned her back towards me and closed her eyes. Now I was annoyed because my dick was hard as hell and she was playing. I knew damn well she wasn't really tired. She was just mad because I told her she couldn't handle Nikki's crazy ass. She would be alright. Too bad I couldn't say the same for Nikki though.

Chapter Five: Reese

Watching Nikki cry over a man that clearly didn't care about her had me feeling some type of way. No, I didn't feel bad for her at all. I told her that she needed to leave him alone and she didn't listen to me. Now she's sad because she's laid up in the hospital. She claims that Rome's girlfriend and some other girls jumped her and hit her in the head with a metal bat, but I didn't know if I believed that or not. They already fought, and his girlfriend beat Nikki's ass, so why would she need to jump her? I keep asking Nikki if that's what really happened, and that's the story she's sticking to.

"Why would he come here and act like he doesn't care about me?" she cried. I tried my hardest not to roll my eyes, but I couldn't help it. She was really starting to get on my nerves with this whole situation.

"Because he doesn't, Nikki." I blurted out. She looked at me like she was shocked, but it was true. Anyone with eyes could see that Rome didn't care about her ass. When I walked in the room, he looked like he was ready to kill her. I didn't know what they were talking about before I walked in, but whatever it was couldn't have been good.

"You don't know that, Reese. If he didn't care about me, he wouldn't have taken me to his house and had sex with me. He wouldn't have taken me to the hospital after his stupid girlfriend beat me up the first time, and he wouldn't have given me a ride home once I got out of the hospital. He didn't even go make sure his girlfriend was okay. He came with me. Then, he came to visit me again today after what his girlfriend has done to me. He cares about me. You just don't want me to be happy." she snapped. I couldn't believe this. She didn't even hear how crazy she sounded right now.

"Nikki, you were nothing more than pussy to him. All I want for you is to be happy, but you can't do that because you're so stuck up Rome's ass who could care less about you."

"You're jealous. That's exactly what it is." I just shook my head at her. Why would I be jealous over her? I got a nigga who actually wants to be my nigga and my nigga only. I'm not chasing after a nigga who is clearly in love with someone else. Speaking of my nigga, I haven't talked to him all day. That's weird because he usually calls me during the day just to see how my day is going.

Pulling out my phone and ignoring Nikki's crazy ass, I dialed Kevin's number. The phone just rang, then eventually went to voicemail. That's weird because he always answers my phone calls. This nigga always answers on the first ring. Maybe he didn't hear his phone. I dialed his number again, but this time, it rang two times and went to voicemail. So now, he was ignoring me? Oh hell no. I decided to call him back one last time, and he finally answered.

"What's going on, sexy?" he said into the phone like he didn't just ignore me two times.

"What are you doing? Why weren't you answering your phone?" I asked.

"Kevin, get off the phone. We can't spend time together while you're on the phone." I heard a woman say in the background. Who the hell was that? Where the hell was he at?

"Aye, I gotta go. I'll holla at you later." he said and hung up the phone before I could even say anything back. Oh, the nerve of this nigga! He had the nerve to rush me off the phone for another bitch? Then the bitch was talking about spending time together and shit? Why the hell did he need to spend time with her ass? He has a whole girlfriend! He needs to be spending time with me, not her.

I took a deep breath because maybe I was overreacting. He did have a sister...Man, hell no. That wasn't his sister's voice at all. I've been around Kaya enough to know her voice, and that voice that I just heard wasn't hers at all. My blood was boiling right now. I wanted to go find that nigga and beat his ass and whoever the chick was too, but I wasn't that type of female though. I didn't fight over men, and I wasn't about to start now. That wasn't who I was.

I stood up and left out of the room without even saying anything to Nikki. I just needed to be alone right now. I almost called Kevin back and cussed his ass out from A to Z, but I decided against it. I would just have to wait until he was done, and he finally called me back.

I knew he was cheating on me. I could feel it. I don't know what it was, but I really felt that shit. I could feel it in the pit of my stomach and it made my chest hurt. I really liked Kevin and he was doing me dirty. It didn't matter how good you were to a nigga, they would never appreciate you. I guess I was learning that the hard way.

I pulled up to my apartment building and turned my car off. I rarely come to my apartment anymore because I'm always with Kevin at his place. I didn't even want to be here right now, but I didn't have anywhere else to go. I didn't want to go to Kevin's place because what if he had the girl over there? I wasn't mentally prepared to walk in on him fucking some other girl. This was just all too much.

I eventually got out of the car and made my way to my apartment. It was so lonely in there and I hated it. It made me think of Kevin and I got mad all over again. I was just stuck wondering who this girl was that was occupying his time right now.

I decided that I was just going to take a nap so that I could stop thinking about him. I wasn't doing anything but making myself sad. I wanted to cry, but I didn't know all of the facts yet. Maybe it was his cousin or something. I doubt that because the only family he had was Kaya, and they weren't really related. I felt so senseless right about now.

***

I could've sworn that I was dreaming, but the banging that was coming from my front door was indeed real. Sitting

48

up in bed, I looked at the clock and saw that I only had been napping for two hours. The banging on the door didn't stop, so I quickly got out of my bed so that I could see who it was at the door. I lived in an apartment complex, not a house, so I could easily get put out because of this.

Swinging the door open, I was face to face with Kevin. He looked mad as hell, and I was confused. Why was he upset? I hadn't done anything to him. He was the one that wanted to be off with other females like he wasn't in a relationship with me.

"Why haven't you been answering your phone?" he said through gritted teeth. I put my phone on silent when I went to bed because I didn't want to be bothered.

"My phone was on silent." I said folding my arms.

"What the fuck you looking at me like that for? You gonna let a nigga in, or what?" Oh, the nerve of this nigga!

"No. I'm not letting you in. How about you go back to whatever bitch's house you were just at." He chortled.

"I wasn't at no bitch's house, Reese." he said looking me directly in the eyes. I didn't mean for it to happen, but my mouth fell open. This man really just lied with a straight face. The worse part was, his lie was believable. It was beyond believable.

"So you're going to sit here and lie to my face?" I had to ask.

"I'm not lying." he said brushing past me and stepping into my apartment. I never invited him in, so why did he feel so comfortable just walking up in here when I'm trying to accuse him of something?

"Then where have you been? Why haven't we talked all day? Why did I hear another woman's voice in the background when I called you earlier, and why did you rush me off the phone for her? Who was she?" I was firing question after question sounding very insecure right now, but I didn't even care. Kevin was trying to play me like I was stupid, and I wasn't about to let that happen. Not now, not ever. He turned to look at me with a smirk on his face. What in the world?

"Why you interrogating me, girl?" he found all of this funny. If I was a violent person, I would probably find something to throw at him. He needed to be hit right now, and I wouldn't even feel bad afterwards either.

"Why are you acting like you aren't in a relationship?"

"I am acting like I'm in a relationship. I came all the way here because you wasn't answering your phone. Now what do you call that?" I closed my eyes and inhaled deeply.

"Who was the girl you were with earlier?" I didn't care about anything else right now. I just wanted to know who he was with and why he was with her. The fact that he hadn't told me about her yet had me feeling like he was real guilty about something. If he wasn't, he would just answer the question, right?

"I wasn't with anyone, Reese. I'm not about to tell your ass no more." Now he's getting defensive? Over a simple question? Yeah, he definitely has something to hide.

"Kevin, I know…" I began to say, but I stopped when I noticed something that shouldn't have gotten my attention at all. Something so simple, yet told me everything that I needed to know. His pants were unzipped. Now, that's something you always remember to zip unless you were rushing.

"What? How are you going to start talking and not finish the sentence?" he had an annoyed tone to his voice. Again, I was taken aback because what the hell was he annoyed about? That he cheated and got caught in the same damn day? I haven't done anything wrong but give his ass another chance. I'm mad at myself for even doing that now.

"Why are your pants unzipped, Kevin?" my voice was low and calm. I felt like I was going to explode at any moment now. He looked down at his pants and quickly tried to zip up his pants. I saw the look of uneasiness in his eyes before he did it too. He was caught and he knew it. After he had zipped up his pants, he made his way into the kitchen and went right into the refrigerator. Now he was avoiding me. Wasn't this some shit?

"So you're just going to ignore me like I didn't ask you a question?" I asked walking up behind him.

"I must've forgot to zip them up before I left the house."

"Get out." I was over it. I was over him and his lies. He was sticking to the lie that he wasn't with a female, when I clearly knew that he was. Why couldn't he just tell me the truth? I obviously didn't mean that much to him in the first place, because if I did, he wouldn't have cheated on me to begin with.

"What?" he seemed shocked that I was actually kicking him out, but I needed him to go. I didn't want to be around him at all anymore. The sight of him was making me sick right now.

"You heard me. I don't need a man that's going to lie to my face. Lying is only making things worse, yet you keep doing it, so please just get out. I don't want you here anymore. I'm tired of you wasting my time." I turned to walk away from him, but he grabbed me by my arm.

"Man, chill. What do you want from me?" he looked so pitiful right now. I snatched my arm from him.

"I just want you to tell me the truth, but you can't seem to do that, so right now, I just want you to leave."

"You want the truth? Aight, I was with my baby mama when you called. I went over there to check on her and shit got outta hand. That's whose voice you heard when we were on the phone. Did I fuck her? Yeah, but did it mean anything to me? Hell no. You're the only girl that means something to me. I realized what I did was fucked up, so I rushed over here." He said all of this like I was just supposed to be okay with it.

"Like I said, you can leave." I wanted to cuss him out, but I couldn't. I couldn't find the words or the voice. I wanted to yell at him, and hit him, and throw things at him, but I couldn't. I had never had this happen to me before. My feelings were never this deep into a relationship like this. I never cared about a man like I cared for Kevin. I knew now that relationships don't mean shit to niggas. At least the white men that I dated took them seriously.

"It's always the same shit with y'all bitches! Y'all beg for the truth, then get it and wanna act all emotional! Don't ask for something you can't handle!" Did he just call me a bitch? First he cheats, now I'm a bitch. It just gets better and better.

"So now I'm a bitch?" I said barely above a whisper. I said it more to myself, but he heard it anyway.

"I didn't mean it like… Man…" he blew out a frustrated breath and stepped closer to me. I took a step back. We didn't need to be that close. He probably still smelled like that bitch, and I didn't want to be that close to him to even find out.

"Just go." I didn't know how many times I was going to have to tell this man to leave. He stared at me for what seemed like forever before he just gave up and finally walked out of my apartment. As soon as he closed the door, I broke down crying. It wasn't one of those quiet, suffer in silence type of cries either. It was ugly, loud, and painful. That feeling in my chest came back. I guess you really can feel it when you get your heart broken. I didn't have any friends that I could just call up and tell to come over because Nikki was still in the hospital, and I'm pretty sure she would find a way to make this about her and Rome. I wasn't tired, but I wanted to go to sleep.

I just wanted the pain that I was feeling to go away. I wanted to go to sleep and wake up tomorrow morning and I didn't want to feel this pain anymore. I wish I would've never met him. I should've just listened to my mom and stuck to white men. I guess that's what I'm going to do from now on because this was just too much for me to handle.

I wasn't much of a drinker, but right now I needed something strong. I wanted a blunt to smoke too, but I didn't know where to get the weed from, and I didn't know how to roll it either. Maybe today could be the day that I learned. *Nah, that's too much damn work. I'll just get me something to drink and call it a day.*

Drying my tears, I walked over to the refrigerator to see what I had to drink in there. Being that I was barely here because I was always at Kevin's, my refrigerator was empty as hell. Ugh. I didn't want to go to the store, but I needed to buy some groceries and maybe I could pick up a bottle of wine on my way home. Make that two bottles. I would probably drink both of the bottles by myself. Damn, I needed some friends.

I grabbed my purse and car keys and made my way out the door. I already planned on calling out of work tomorrow because I was drinking all night so I already knew that I was going to have a mean ass hangover in the morning. I might not even get out of bed at all tomorrow either.

Looking down at my phone as I walked to my car, I immediately regretted it when I ran into something hard causing my phone to fall to the ground and shatter the screen.

"Shit." I mumbled.

"Damn, my bad, Ma. I should've been watching where I was going." a male voice said. I looked up at him and thought I was dreaming. There was no way possible that this man that I was staring at was real. He bent down to pick up my phone and handed it to me.

"I…" I tried to say but my tongue was paralyzed right now. I couldn't say a thing. All I could do was stare at this fine ass white man like I didn't have any sense.

"Shidd, I ain't even mean to break ya phone. If you want, I can buy you another one." he said. *What the hell?* He didn't look like he would talk like that at all. He was tall as hell, probably about 6'3, he had long brown hair, but it was up in a man bun that a lot of white men wear nowadays, and he had piercing blue eyes. I felt like he was looking into my soul with those things.

"N-no, it's okay." I said fumbling over my words.

"Nah, nah. Let me get it fixed for you. That's the least I could do since I'm the one that made you drop it." He smiled at me showing his perfect, straight, white teeth. His sexiness was on a whole different level.

"No really, it's okay." I tried to let him know, but he wasn't taking no for an answer.

"I live right there in that apartment. You could come in and wait for me while I change clothes or you can wait out here for me. Your choice." he said. I didn't know this man from a can of paint, so I didn't understand why my legs had a mind of their own and decided to follow behind him. I still hadn't even gotten his name yet. I didn't even know that he lived two doors down from me. I guess it was because I didn't really pay attention to anyone while I was here.

Stepping into his apartment behind him, it didn't even look like anyone lived here. There wasn't any kind of furniture in the living room, there weren't any dishes in the sink, and it was so dull and boring in there. There weren't any pictures or anything hanging up on the wall. No decorations whatsoever.

"I won't be long." he said. I didn't understand why he had to change clothes until I looked at what he was wearing. He wore an all-black, long sleeved shirt, and all black pants. He even went as far as having on all black Timberland boots too. That made me wonder what the hell he was doing before I ran into him. It's hot as hell in Atlanta and he was wearing long sleeves? Nah, something wasn't right.

I stood by the door awkwardly as he went in the room that was located in the back to change clothes. It would've been nice to sit down, but I couldn't for obvious reasons. I couldn't do anything but stand here and wait for him. I wish he would've just let me go on about my day. My phone was the least of my worries right now. I could always get that fixed later on. As long as I was still able to call people on it, I was good.

About five minutes later, he walked out of the room wearing a pair of denim jeans and a plain black shirt. I could see all of the tattoos that decorated his arms and that went up to his neck. I was almost certain that he had even more tattoos all over his chest too. His outfit was so simple, but he looked so good. His hair was still up in his man bun that I was finding very attractive right about now.

"Aight, let's go. I got some shit I need to get into later." he said walking past me and out the door. His scent hit me in the face as he walked by. He smelled lovely.

"Are you going to tell me your name?" I asked once we got into his car. He was driving an all-black Range Rover. It was seeming like his favorite color was black or something.

"You can call me Jay." he said without even looking at me.

"Is that your real name?"

"It's what you can call me." Rude ass. I didn't say anything else to him because I was just ready for all of this to be over. I wanted to go to the store, get what I needed for the night, then take my ass home, but he was making things so damn difficult. All he had to do was apologize and keep it moving. I didn't need all of this extra shit that he was doing.

It was awkward as hell in his car. He wasn't talking to me, and I wasn't talking to him. The radio wasn't even on. He still hadn't asked me for my name either. He's so rude, but he was so fine. You could tell he wasn't just a regular white boy that you come across. He reminded me of Kevin. I wished he didn't though.

"Why you staring at me like that?" he asked startling me. I didn't even realize that I was staring at him that hard, and now I was caught. "I know I look good and shit, but damn." He smiled cockily, and I rolled my eyes.

"I wasn't." was all I could think to say. He chuckled lightly.

"There's no need to lie. I know I look good. Bitches let me know all the time." He was still smiling, and it was annoying. I wasn't about to give him the satisfaction.

"Maybe if you cut your hair and didn't have all of those tattoos, I would find you attractive. Your eyes are pretty though." I was lying through my teeth. Everything thing about him was very attractive.

"Maybe if you didn't have that annoying ass, squeaky voice, I would find you attractive." My mouth fell open. I knew he was rude, but damn. I didn't think my voice was annoying or squeaky. Was it? I didn't have a comeback for him. What he had just said shut my ass up the whole way to the Apple Store.

"How much do you think this shit is about to cost?" he asked. I smacked my lips.

"If you couldn't afford it, then you shouldn't have even offered to pay for it." I said with my voice laced with attitude.

He looked at me like I had just insulted him, then burst out into a fit of laughter. I didn't know what the hell he thought was so funny. He dug into his pocket and pulled out a wad of money. He took the rubber band off then threw all of the money in my face.

"Does money look like a problem for me, Ma?" He was still laughing, and I was livid. Who the fuck did this man think he was? I reacted out of anger and hit him in the back of his head.

"Don't you ever throw your money in my face like I'm just some hoe in a strip club or some shit! I don't care how much money you got!" I snapped. He had a shocked look on his face. I guess he didn't expect me to hit him. Well, I didn't expect him to throw his money in my face either.

"Don't put your hands on me, girl." he said.

"My name is Reese. Your rude ass offered to buy me a new phone, but you couldn't even ask what my name is." I shook my head and grabbed the handle to the door. "Don't even worry about it. You don't have to pay for my phone; I'll do it myself!" I got out of his car and made sure I slammed the door hard as hell. I was mad that I even ran into him earlier. He wasn't making my day any better. I started walking down the street. I didn't even care anymore.

"Aye!" I heard him yell after me. I ignored him and kept it moving. I had no idea how I was going to get back to my apartment building, but I was going to try my best. "Aye, I know you hear me calling you!" I stopped walking and turned around to look at him. He was jogging up to me with one hand holding his pants up.

"What?" I asked while folding my arms.

"Let me buy you a new phone so I can drop your ass back off. You being real extra right now." he had the nerve to say.

"I'm being real extra? You started this shit by throwing that dirty ass money in my face like you don't have any sense! I don't need you to buy me anything. I'm good. I'll find a way home." I turned to walk off again, but he grabbed me by my arm and start dragging me the direction that the Apple Store was in.

"Let me go!" I hollered.

"Man, shut the hell up! Let me do what I said I was going to do." Onlookers were staring at us like we were crazy. I'm pretty sure that's exactly how we looked.

"I said no!"

"Ma'am, are you alright?" an older man, who was standing on the sidewalk asked me.

"She's good my man! Mind ya fucking business!" Jay yelled at the man. I was so embarrassed right now. There was nothing I could do either, because he had a death grip on my damn arm.

By the time we got inside of the Apple Store, his face was red as hell, and he looked like he was ready to blow the whole store up if someone didn't help us soon.

"Aye, can somebody help me or not?" he yelled out. I just dropped my head in shame because I was that embarrassed. Everyone in the store was staring at us and the workers even looked afraid to come and help us.

"What can I do for you today?" A female asked from behind us. She was white and eyeing the fuck out of Jay. If he was my man, I would probably be feeling some type of way right now.

"I got a phone that needs to be fixed. You know what, fuck all that. Just give me a new one." This man really didn't know how to talk to people.

"What kind of phone?" she asked.

"Shit, I don't know. Aye, show her what kind of phone you got." He demanded. I took my phone out of my back pocket and handed it to the girl. She snatched it out of my hand and rolled her eyes at me. She didn't even know that I wouldn't hesitate to put my hands on her. I don't even care that this is her place of work.

"I'll be right back." she muttered before walking off. Jay and I just stood there awkwardly not knowing what to say to each other. It seemed like this girl was taking her sweet little time on purpose, and I was just ready to go. I didn't even want to go to the grocery store anymore. I'll just order me some shit and call it a night.

"Look uh… I shouldn't have threw my money in your face like that earlier. I…I got ahead of myself, and I shouldn't have done that." he said.

"Yeah, that was rude as hell." I let him know.

"I know that. I'm not used to dealing with bitches… I mean women like you. I…umm… apologize." He was stumbling over his words, and I thought it was cute. I knew he was nervous, because his face was red as hell.

"Just don't let it happen again." I said. The girl finally came back with my new phone and I couldn't have been happier. I was so ready to take my ass home.

After she rung everything up, she told us what the total was and Jay paid for everything in cash.

"You're a really good looking guy. It was nice of you to buy your *friend* a new phone." she said. I was about to say something to this little bitch, but Jay beat me to it.

"Thanks for the compliment, but you're wasting your time. You're a little too pale for my liking. You see my *friend* right here?" he asked pointing to me. "That's what I like. I need a girl like her with a lot of ass that I can grab on. Have a nice day though." He winked at her, and we walked out of the store. Now I had a new phone with no one's number in it. Great.

When he pulled up to the apartment building, I was happy as hell. Today just hasn't been my day at all. I just wanted to cuddle with my pillow and call it a night. I was still wishing I had something strong to drink.

"I guess I'll see you around, Ma." he said as I got out of his car.

"Yeah, I guess so." I closed his door and made my way to my apartment. Today has been very interesting, and I was just glad that it was about to be over.

.

Chapter Six: Kevin

After I walked out of Reese's apartment, I just stood by her door for a minute. I could hear her crying and shit and that bothered me. I didn't want her to be crying, and I damn sure didn't want to be the reason that she was crying. Shit was all fucked up right now and it was all my fault. I brought all of this on myself.

I decided that I needed to check up on Amaya because I hadn't talked to her in a little minute. I know I said I didn't want anything to do with her, but just in case the baby does turn out to be mine, I want to make sure she's good. All I really had to do was call her and see what was up with her, but my dumb ass just had to go by her crib and shit. That was probably the worst thing that I could've done, because as soon as she saw me, she was all over me.

She had her hands down my pants and was kissing on my neck and shit. I had a weak moment. I didn't even realize that I was ignoring Reese's calls until she called back the third time. Her calling should've been enough for me to leave Amaya's place and take my ass to wherever she was, but I couldn't though.

As I was trying to talk to Reese over the phone, Amaya said some shit about spending time together, then I felt my dick touch the back of her throat. She knew exactly what she was doing. I had to hurry up and get off the phone before I moaned out like a little bitch. Her head game was lethal, and she knew it.

Now my ass is over here looking sick as fuck because I got caught. I want to be mad at Amaya, but I couldn't be. She didn't force me to fuck her all over her crib. That was all my doing. I was thinking with the wrong head, and now my girl doesn't want anything to do with me. Crazy right? After Amaya fucked up everything the first time with Reese, one would think that I would stop fucking with her right? Wrong.

"You look so sad. What's the matter?" I heard Kaya ask walking down the stairs with a box in her hand.

"Not shit." was all I said. I didn't want her to know about what had happened today. She would probably have a lot to say about it, and I wasn't in the mood for that at all.

"The lies you tell. I know it has something to do with Reese though." she said sitting her box down by the door, then walking back up the stairs. How the hell did she know that it had something to do with Reese? Maybe Reese called her and told her about what I did. I doubt that because they didn't really talk like that. She came back down the stairs with another box in her hand. She looked at me and chuckled.

"Stop looking like that, nigga." she said.

"How do you know that it has something to do with Reese?" I had to ask. I hope Reese wasn't out here telling all of our business and shit.

"Because you down here sitting in the damn dark looking like you've lost your best friend and shit. Before you started messing with Reese, you were never sad. Knowing you, you done some fucked up shit to that girl and now she doesn't want anything to do with you." I didn't say anything back to her because she was right. I wish she wasn't though. I wish I could go back in time and make today not even happen. Amaya should be the last thing that I'm worried about.

"If I would've known that you were here, I would've asked you to help me pack my things." she said.

"Pack your things for what? You going on a trip or some shit?"

"Hell no, nigga. I'm moving the hell out. It's been real and everything, but I need my own space. Plus, I'm tired of hearing you and Reese have sex at night." She said pretending to throw up.

"I hear you and Royal fucking all the time; you don't see me complaining though."

"Boy bye! You stay banging on my damn door like you're the police or some shit. You need your own space, and I need mine. I think it's for the best." I wasn't feeling this at all.

"Where the hell are you moving to? How much does it cost? What side of town is it on? Why you just now telling me about this?" she rolled her eyes at me.

"Damn Kevin, chill. It's like ten minutes away from here, and it's an apartment. I didn't think I needed something big because it's just going to be me living there. Now I can walk around naked if I really wanted to." she smiled. I just shook my head at her.

"You're moving in today?"

"Yep. I can't wait either. This is going to be so great." I didn't want her to move out, but the idea seemed to make her happy, so I was okay with it. I didn't want to tell her what she could and couldn't do, because at the end of the day, she was going to do what she wanted anyway. It's been that way ever since I met her when she was sixteen.

"I ain't helping yo' big headed ass so don't even ask." I joked. She knew I was lying so she didn't even bother to say anything about it.

"What did you do to Reese?" I didn't want to talk about Reese right now. The only thing that I wanted was for Reese to talk to me. I had been blowing up her phone since I left. She finally got tired of hitting the ignore button and just turned her phone all the way off. I hated how I felt without her. Knowing she didn't want anything to do with me was really fucking with my head.

"Cheated." I didn't even go into detail about what I had done. There was no point. I did what I did, and I lost Reese because of it.

"Niggas." Kaya said shaking her head at me.

"She won't even answer my phone calls. She's not a violent person like you. I don't know how she handles situations like this. She was crying hard as hell when I left too." I shook my head thinking about earlier.

"Of course she's not going to answer the phone! It just happened. You gotta give her some time."

"What did you do when Royal cheated on you? Did you give him some time? Are y'all two good now?" She twisted her face up.

"Fuck him. No we're not good. We never will be good. I have nothing to say to him and that's that. I wasn't enough for him, so I'm going to keep doing what I was doing. Relationships don't mean shit to niggas nowadays, so why should I even waste my time?" She sounded pretty confident about being done with Royal, but I know for a fact that I saw that nigga leaving out of here the other night.

"So you're done with that nigga?" I asked with a raised eyebrow.

"Beyond done." Just as she said that, her phone began to ring, and she looked down at it. Rolling her eyes, she hit the ignore button and looked at me. I knew it was that nigga Royal calling. I also knew my sister. She claims she's done with him, but I know she's not. Her feelings are still hurt right now.

"Stop looking at me like that and help me bring the rest of my boxes down here." she said getting off the couch and walking back up the stairs. Being the good big brother that I am, I got off of the couch and followed right behind her. Maybe helping her move out would keep my mind off of Reese for a while. Shit, I sure hoped it did.

Kaya's new apartment was actually nice as hell. It looked like it cost a pretty penny, but I'm sure she could handle it since she wanted to be all independent all of a sudden. I was starting to think she had way more money than she claimed she did, because there was brand new furniture in the apartment already. The bed that she had at my house was perfectly fine, but she went out and bought a whole new one.

"Why didn't you just take the bed that you already had at my house?" I asked bringing her boxes into the apartment. She was just sitting on the couch scrolling through her phone. She wasn't even trying to help a nigga out.

"Because I fucked Royal in that bed and now I want nothing to do with it." she said without even looking up at me. I looked at her with disgust written all over my face. I was now regretting that I even asked.

"So basically, you just wasted money on a new bed for no reason."

"No nigga, I had a reason and I just told you what it was. Now less talking and more moving these boxes." She didn't even look up at me when she said that. She better be glad that I loved her little ass, because I would've just left and made her do the rest by herself.

Once I was back outside getting some more boxes, Reese popped in my head. I tried my hardest not to think about her, but it wasn't working at all. It was going to be hard as hell, but maybe I should give her some space like Kaya said. My phone started ringing bringing me out of my thoughts of Reese.

"You did it again! Why do you keep fucking me and acting like I don't mean shit to you?!" Brandi yelled into the phone before I could even say anything. This was annoying as hell. She knew exactly how I was, yet she continued to fuck with me.

"I don't know how many times I have to tell you that you don't mean shit to me before you actually understand that shit. You know what it is, so if you can't handle it, then get the fuck off my line and go fuck with another nigga."

"Do you tell that Reese bitch that you don't care about her like that? You be parading her around town like she's the baddest bitch out here. You can do so much better, Kevin." I chuckled. Females were always hating on the next chick.

"Calling her a bitch won't change the situation between us. In my eyes, she is the baddest bitch out here. How you even know who she is anyway? You stalking me or some shit? You didn't seem like the type of bitch to stalk a nigga when I first started fucking with you, but it seems like I was obviously wrong."

"Nigga please! I know Reese because of my dad. Ain't nobody stalking you. Don't flatter yourself because your dick ain't even good enough for me to stalk your ass. You fucking wish." I couldn't help the smile that spread across my face.

"Oh word? Then, why the hell you call me complaining about me fucking you and cutting your ass off? Then you got the nerve to be talking to me about another female. You sound like a hater to me." I laughed.

"I am far from a hater, Kevin. Plus, your little girlfriend Reese made a status saying how she's done with black men and sticking to the white boys. Sounds to me like she's not fucking with your ass anymore."

Brandi started laughing like this shit was funny. There wasn't shit funny about what the hell she had just told me. I know I hurt Reese and shit, but she didn't have to go and make a status like that. She just gonna put it out there that she's single? There's probably hella niggas in her inbox right now hoping to get a chance. My blood was boiling right now. Just thinking about niggas trying to get with her had me ready to kill any and everything walking.

"What's the matter, Kevin? You thought she was the one for you didn't you? Nope. She likes white men. Always has and always will." Brandi said laughing even harder. I think she was getting a kick out of this.

"Damn Brandi. I started fucking with you because you didn't seem like one of those money hungry, ratchet bitches that talk shit about everybody, but boy was I wrong. I ain't fucking with you no more like that. Lose my number and act like you don't know me when you see me out in public."

"Kevin, wai—" she tried to say but I hung up on her stupid ass before she could even say anything else. I really did think she was different from all of the other bitches that I've been fucking with. She seemed classy and she made her own money. I guess just because she wore glasses and acted professionally at work didn't mean shit. She was just like the others and I didn't want to fuck with her like that anymore.

Brandi called right back, but I didn't answer. I sent her ass straight to voicemail. She and I didn't have anything to talk about. I was glad that she let me know about that stupid shit Reese put on the Internet, but at the same time, I was mad as hell. I wanted to go straight to Reese's house and cuss her ass out, but I kept remembering that I was the one that fucked up and I was still trying to give her some space. I would show up at her place tomorrow. One day is enough alone time for her, right?

***

"Have you had enough to eat?" Amaya asked as I sat on her couch.

"Yeah, I'm good." I know I shouldn't even be over here right now, but a nigga's dick is hard, and I know I can get some head with no questions asked from her.

"So what do you think our baby will look like? I hope he or she comes out looking just like you." She smiled.

"Yeah, if it's mine, it might look like me." I could tell by the look on her face that she didn't like what I said at all. I didn't care though. She had a boyfriend when I started fucking around with her. She claims I'm the only nigga that she was fucking, but I don't believe that shit at all.

"Stop saying that shit, Kevin. You know this baby is yours." She rolled her eyes and flipped her weave over her shoulder.

"Nah, I won't know shit until that DNA test comes back." I knew she was about to try and start an argument, and that's not what I was here for. "You sucking my dick, or nah?" I asked.

"Is that the only reason you came over here? So that you could get some head?" she asked with an attitude.

"No, I came to eat too." I said smiling at her. She folded her arms and pouted. She was doing too much right now. I just wanted my dick sucked so that I could take my ass home.

"You're just using me, Kevin." I blew out a frustrated breath.

"Man, whatever. I'll find another bitch to do it." I said standing up.

"Wait, no. I didn't mean any of that." She dropped to her knees and started unbuckling my pants. That's what the fuck I thought. All I have to do is mention another bitch around her, and she's going to start acting right. She should be acting right in the first place.

Once she started doing her thing, all I could think about was Reese. This should be Reese right now in this position with my dick down her throat. She's never given me head before so I already knew that it probably wouldn't be as good as Amaya's, but it could get there one day.

Gripping the back of Amaya's head while she acted like she didn't have a gag reflex had my toes curling. If things were different, and Amaya wasn't crazy, I would marry her just because of her head game alone. This shit should be illegal.

"Fuck." I muttered trying my hardest to keep my moans to myself. I didn't want to sound like a little bitch in here, but it was getting hard not to. She was even moaning like she was getting pleasure out of this. She looked at me the entire time, never breaking eye contact. This would be a thousand times better if it was Reese that I was looking down at right now. That's when the thought of Reese fucking with some lame ass white boy popped in my head and my dick instantly went limp.

"What the fuck, Kevin?" Amaya asked.

"Man, I gotta go. I'll hit you up later or some shit." I said fixing my dick in my pants then heading towards the door.

"Kevin, wait! How you just gonna leave like this?" she called from behind me. I ignored her though. I just needed to leave. I was tempted to just show up at Reese's place, but I was determined to wait until tomorrow. I needed to calm down anyway. I didn't want to just show up at her apartment and then go off on her for making that status. I needed to let her know how sorry I was about fucking up—again. I just hope she will actually hear me out this time. I got to do better with the decisions I make.

Chapter Seven: Kaya

Being in my own apartment felt good as hell. I was walking around naked just because I could. I was glad that Kevin helped me get settled in, because I didn't have anyone else to help, and I didn't want to pay someone else to do it for me. The best part of having my own place was Royal not knowing where I lived. I hated how he thought that he could just pop up on me whenever he felt like it. It didn't work like that at all. I still didn't want anything to do with him even though I was missing him something terrible right now.

I hadn't let him talk to me, because I already knew that I would give in to him, and most likely, he would have me face down ass up somewhere like he's been doing for the past couple of days. I know what you're thinking. Why am I still fucking Royal if I'm claiming that I don't want anything to do with him? Well, it's simple. His dick game is way too good for me to just give that up. I was good with just fucking him. No words needed to be spoken between us. He would just show up at the house, and he knew exactly what I wanted. Then, after we finished, I would kick his ass out before he could even try talking to me about our relationship.

"Bitch, why couldn't you be normal and get your apartment on the first floor like normal damn people?" Clay asked, as we talked on the phone. She was complaining because my apartment was on the second floor. She would be okay though.

"Girl, you need some damn exercise. Stop complaining." I said hearing a knock at my door. I knew it was probably just Clay since she was on her way up here.

"Shut the hell up. I'm sore as hell. You should've came and picked me up instead of me driving." Getting up to open the door, I was shocked as hell that Clay wasn't standing there. I was even more shocked that this nigga even knew where I lived at.

"What the fuck." I said to myself.

"What? What happened?" Clay asked. I hung up the phone and thought about slamming the door in his face. I guess he knew what I was about to do because he stepped into my apartment and closed the door behind him.

"Royal, what the hell are you doing here? How do you even know that I live here?" I asked. He didn't look like he was too happy to see me at all. In fact, he looked like he wanted to strangle my ass. I didn't know why, but damn he was looking good as hell. I don't know what it was about a man in a suit but I was getting wet just looking at him. *Damn.* He had his dreads braided back in two braids, and from the looks of it, he dyed the ends back black. Was it possible that him having all black dreads was making him look even better? Hmm…

"I'm getting tired of this shit, Kay." he said.

"Getting tired of what shit?" I played dumb like I didn't know what he was talking about. I knew exactly what he was talking about though.

"You know what the fuck I'm talking about. I'm not about to keep fucking you and you can't even talk to me like a fucking adult!" I felt like a terrible person right now. Here he is yelling about me fucking him and not giving him a chance to talk to me, and that's exactly what I wanted to do. He was looking way too good for me to be able to have a conversation with him right now. I wonder if he did that on purpose. He knew he was looking like a walking god right now.

"Kay!" he said getting my attention, because I was too busy lusting over him.

"Huh?"

"You're not even listening to me, bruh." He was shaking his head and looking at me like I disgusted him. I hated when he called me bruh, and he knew it. I wasn't a man so don't call me bruh. I rolled my eyes as Clay walked into the apartment. She had the same look on her face that I did when I saw Royal standing at the door.

"Is this a bad time?" she asked looking at me with a raised eyebrow.

"Nah, I ain't gonna be long at all. I just need to talk to your friend real quick." he said walking in the direction of my room. I knew he wanted me to follow him, but I was still stuck on the fact that he knew where I lived already. It hasn't even been a week.

"Are y'all back together?" Clay whispered. I shook my head no as I started to walk to my room where Royal was waiting for me. He was sitting on my bed with his suit jacket off. He looked like he was stressing, but what could he possibly be stressing about?

"So how do you know where I live at?" I asked standing at the door with my arms folded. He looked at up me and smirked.

"It hurts my feelings that you still don't know what your man is capable of." he chuckled.

"I…Umm…You're not my man." I said staring at all the gold that was in his mouth. He didn't say anything. He just got up off the bed and shut the door. This nigga even had the nerve to lock it too. I already knew what was on his mind from the way he kept looking at my body and licking his lips. I did look good in my gray leggings that I was wearing with no underwear and a white tank top. Outfit so simple, yet I looked like a model. Not trying to brag or anything.

"How long you gonna keep ignoring a nigga?" he asked loosening his tie.

"I'm not ignoring you. I don't want anything to do with you. Not now, not ever."

"Straight up?" I nodded my head knowing damn well I was lying. He moved so that he was standing right in front of me. He was so close, I could smell the mint that was on his breath. Knowing his ass, he probably chewed a whole pack of gum before he got here.

He started kissing on my neck knowing he was making me weak as hell. I bit the insides of my cheek to keep from moaning out. I didn't want him to know that he was making me feel good. He didn't deserve to know that right now. He didn't deserve me period. I'm not good enough for him to keep his dick to himself, so why was he here in my room trying to get me to come back—

"Oh shit." I whispered once I felt his hand in my pants playing with what no longer belonged to him. I didn't expect it at all, but I didn't want him to stop either.

"You gonna talk to me, Kaya?" he whispered in my ear. I hated him. I hated the effect he had on my body, and I damn sure hated how he had me about to cum without even sticking a finger inside of me.

"No." I moaned. He pulled his hand from in my pants and took a step back. I looked at him like he was crazy.

"You ain't getting no dick until you talk to me, since you wanna be childish and shit." He let me know. No this nigga didn't. Him saying that was enough to make my ass start crying.

"What? Are you serious right now?" I said louder than I intended too. He didn't say anything. He turned to walk to my bed and grabbed his suit jacket. Was he serious? It was looking like he was serious as hell.

"You got my number. Hit me up when you're ready to be an adult." he said and walked out of my room leaving me standing there looking stupid and feeling horny as hell. I heard the front door open and close, and I couldn't do anything but stand there. This wasn't fair. He was acting like I was the one that did something wrong. Why the hell was he punishing me? He was the one that was caught with another bitch in his bed.

"Close your mouth before a fly gets in it." Clay said standing at the door. I didn't even know that my mouth was open, but I was still in shock about what just happened.

"The nerve of this nigga." I said to myself.

"What happened? When did he get here?" she asked. I know she wanted answers, but I couldn't focus right now. I walked past her and into the kitchen. I sat down on the table where the pack of Black n Mild's were sitting and picked it up.

"Kaya?" Clay said following me. *Where's my damn lighter?* I looked all around the kitchen and noticed that it was sitting on the counter next to the sink. I quickly grabbed it so I could light this damn black.

"Bitch, you're going to stop ignoring me and tell me what the hell he said to you." Clay said sitting down at the table in front of me. She looked at the pack of Black n Mild's that were on the table and turned her nose up.

"Don't start, Clay. I don't even want to hear it." I said blowing out a cloud of smoke.

"Fine. When you get addicted to them nasty shits again, don't come crying to me." she said. I rolled my eyes. I've always had a problem with smoking cigarettes and Black n Milds. I could stop for a little bit, but I would end up just smoking again like now. I only needed them when I was stressed as hell, but I had a hard time putting them down once I started again. Kevin and Clay hated it. They would always talk shit when I smoked around them, and it was annoying. I didn't care though. They didn't know what was going on in my damn head.

"Now tell me what happened." she said.

"Well, he basically just came over to talk. I don't know how the hell he even knows where I live at, but he does. I didn't want to talk to him, so he said I can't get no dick until I stop being childish and talk to him." I still couldn't believe this. I felt like he was punishing me for something that he did.

"Well, that's not going to be hard for you. You've been ignoring him anyway." I forgot that I hadn't told her that I was still fucking Royal. I looked down at my fingers then back up at her.

"Yeah, I've been ignoring him… with my face down and ass up."

"What? What the hell are you talking about?" she was chuckling, but she didn't get what I was saying.

"We've been fucking almost every night." I said quietly.

"Kaya, what the fuck?!" she yelled.

"I can't help it! His dick is way too good for me to just let some other bitch have it. It's like a drug that I need." I finished the Black that I was smoking and instantly lit another one.

"Stop playing with that man and take him back. It's obvious you still want him. Why are you trying to put on this tough girl front?"

"I don't want him. I don't want a nigga that can't keep his dick in his pants. I deserve better." Clay rolled her eyes.

"All men cheat, Kaya. I know you probably don't want to hear that right now, but it's the truth. I think you should give him another chance. If he fucks up again, then you leave his ass. Rome has one last time with me before I'm done with him." I didn't want to give Royal a second chance. I didn't think he deserved one. If I would've cheated and he caught me, he probably would've killed me and whoever the nigga was that I cheated on him with.

"I don't know." was all I said back. If I took him back, he would think it's okay to cheat on me again, and I couldn't have that. I would definitely end up killing his ass this time. He's lucky that I didn't do it when I killed Roxy.

"Just think on it. I support you with whatever you do." she let me know. That's why she was my bitch.

Clay and I talked for hours and watched movies on TV. Well, really the TV was watching us because we were so into our conversation to even pay attention to it. I ended up smoking the whole pack of Black n Mild's, and of course, she had something to say about it. I was supposed to be sleep because I was going to work tonight, but I would rather talk to Clay since I barely saw her when she was in the hospital. I wanted to find that Nikki bitch myself and put my hands on her, but Clay insisted that she's gonna be able to handle it. I didn't think she was going to be able to do it by herself though.

"I still can't believe that Erica's scary ass actually helped you." I said scrolling through my phone.

"Girl me either, but I'm glad she did. I probably would've lost my mind if that bitch would've made me lose my baby. That's something I never want to go through. I don't know how people just go on with their life and act like they didn't lose a part of them." I looked up at her and she was shaking her head. She didn't even know that she was making me sad talking about this.

"Yeah, me either." I quietly said. She looked at me with a confused look on her face before she realized why I was sad.

"Oh my gosh! I'm sorry. I didn't mean to bring it up…" she said with her voice trailing off.

"It's okay. You didn't do it on purpose." I couldn't help but wonder what I would've looked like pregnant. I still can't even imagine my tummy getting huge, getting stretch marks, or being sick all the time, but I knew in the end it would all be worth it when I met my sweet baby. Too bad I would never know the feeling though.

"I need a pack of cigarettes." I mumbled to myself. Clay looked at me with a scowl on her face. I didn't care though. I was still going to get me a pack.

"Kaya, those things are going to kill you." I waved her off and got off the couch.

"I'll be okay, I promise." Looking at the time, it was starting to get late and I hadn't been to sleep at all. I was going to be tired, but I was taking my ass to work tonight. I had to make money some kind of way because I didn't want to rob anyone anymore. At least not right now…

Hours later, Clay had gone home to her man, while I drove to the club ready to get this money. My weave was curled to perfection, my makeup looked like it was done professionally, and as always, my body would put anyone's to shame. I knew I was looking good, and I was definitely feeling myself. Royal was the last thing on my mind right now. He wanted to play? Well, I could play the game way better than him.

On the way to the club, I remembered that I didn't have any cigarettes, so I stopped at the nearest gas station to get some. Pulling into the pump like I was about to get gas, I quickly got out the car and made my way into the store. I hated this gas station because there were always people standing out front begging for money. Then when you told them no, they get mad at you like it's your fault they're out there begging to begin with.

"Excuse me miss, do you have a quarter?" an old black man asked that was standing right by the door. See what I mean?

"Nope." I said, without even looking at him, while keeping it moving into the store. Of course he didn't believe me and followed me right into the store. I kept pepper spray and a .45 in my purse for niggas like him. He better leave me the hell alone.

"You in the store about to buy something, but you can't give me a quarter?" he asked following behind me.

"I know one thing, you better back the hell up off of me if you know what's good for you." I snapped. Why couldn't people just take no as an answer? I hurried and walked up to the counter and asked for two packs of cigarettes. I needed more than this, but these two would have to do right now.

"I see you got money in your purse." he said standing all close to me still.

"Nigga, back the fuck up! I said I don't have any money to give you, damn!" I yelled snatching my cigarettes off the counter and storming out of the store. Of course he was still right behind me. I didn't have time for this at all.

"Well, why you can't just give me a dollar instead of the quarter. I see you got plenty of those." He grabbed me by my arm and I lost it. I pulled the pepper spray out and sprayed him in both of his eyes. He had me so fucked up.

"Ahhh!" he screamed out and fell to the ground holding his face. I didn't feel bad for him at all. Instead of being out here begging and shit, he needed to be out trying to get a damn job. Bum ass nigga. I quickly got into my car and sped off. For some reason, my mind drifted to Royal. He would've killed that nigga with no questions asked. Especially after seeing the old man try and put his hands on me. Damn, I miss that nigga.

Pulling up to the club, I suddenly got a bad feeling in the pit of my stomach. I didn't know what it was, but I didn't like it at all. I was debating on whether I should go in or listen to my gut and take my ass home. I pulled out a cigarette and lit it. It might just be my nerves messing with me. I sure hope it was just my nerves.

I got out the car and made my way into the club. There weren't many people in there yet, but that was only because it was still early. Soon, this place would be packed with niggas ready to spend their money on me. That's the only thing that kept me at this job.

"What's good, Kaya? You ready to make some money tonight?" the club owner Mario asked as he eyed my body and licked his lips. He's always had a thing for me, but I just didn't see myself messing with him on that level. He was about ten years older than me and was about his money. He was fine as hell, there was no denying that, but he just wasn't my type.

"I'm always ready to make money." I winked at him as I walked to the locker room. Girls were already back there putting on makeup and curling their hair. It was like as soon as I entered the room, everyone stopped and looked at me. They were acting like I was someone famous or something. I guess I was when it came to this club. I was the best dancer up in this bitch.

"Ask her where Roxy is." I heard someone say as I made my way to my locker. I rolled my eyes. This is why I didn't have any friends here. All bitches did was hate on the next woman and gossip. Why did they think I had something to do with Roxy's disappearance? Even though I did, that's still none of their damn business.

"She probably doesn't know. I know Roxy was fucking Royal though. She was at his house the last time I talked to her." this girl named Cherry said. I guess she thought she was whispering, but she wasn't. I could hear everything loud and clear, and this was a conversation that was definitely pissing me off. First off, they shouldn't be talking about Royal. Secondly, Roxy should've listened to me and left Royal alone. She would've lived much longer if she would've listened.

"Kaya, have you heard from Roxy? She hasn't been to work lately, and a few of us are starting to get worried." Cherry said to me. I looked up at her debating if I wanted to cuss her stupid ass out or not.

"Why the hell would I know where Roxy is?" I asked.

"Well because you were with Royal and she told me that she was—" I cut her stupid ass off.

"Was that bitch my friend? Did I hang out with her at all? When the hell did I ever talk to her? The better question is, why the fuck are you even approaching me about another bitch?" The whole locker room went silent as they waited for Cherry to respond to me. She twisted her face up and folded her arms across her fake ass titties.

"I was just asking a question because she was fucking your man. Don't get mad at me because your nigga ain't faithful." she said rolling her neck. I guess she thought she was doing something by letting me know about Roxy and Royal, but little did she know, I was the reason Roxy was no longer with us.

"You done?" I asked with a light chuckle.

"Do you know where she is? Yes or no?" I didn't know who the fuck Cherry thought she was talking to, but she was about to catch these hands. She needed to get out my face if she knew what was best for her.

"Bitch, do it look like I know where your friend is? Instead of interrogating me, you need to be worried about if you're going to make any money today with that fake ass you got that doesn't move. Get the fuck out my face before you get me fired, hoe." Cherry just stared at me with wide eyes. I knew what kind of female she was. She was all bark and no bite. She would run her mouth, but wouldn't fight at all. I couldn't stand females like that. Shit was so annoying.

"Damn, she just punked her ass." I heard someone say with a laugh. I continued to ignore everyone as I got ready for the night. Hopefully, no one else would try me on some stupid shit like Cherry did.

The club was packed just like I expected it to be. That alone made me smile as I made my way to the bar so that I could get me a drink. I just wanted to have a little buzz before I went up on stage.

"Damn girl, you should come visit me in my section." some man said grabbing my arm. I turned to look at him and I was instantly turned off. You could tell that he was nothing but a show-off. Whatever little money he did get, he spent it on stupid shit just so he could look cool in front of his friends. He had on Gucci from head to toe looking dumb as hell because he obviously didn't know how to match. He had so many gold chains around his neck, it didn't make any sense. There was no way in hell he needed all those damn chains on. He even had on two Rolexes, one on each wrist. It was never that serious.

"I'll be sure to do that." I said giving him a fake smile. As much as I didn't want to, he was probably going to be throwing hella money, and I knew for a fact I wasn't about to miss out on that. He smiled back and made his way back to his section. I could tell his ass was drunk, so I already knew that I could have some fun with him. Not what kind of fun y'all are thinking though.

My performance was one for the books, as always. It went by pretty quick, and I was happy about that. I just wasn't feeling tonight at all. I grabbed my money and made my way to the locker room, but I was stopped on the way by the same nigga who asked me to come to his section earlier.

"You still coming to my section right? You should bring a friend." He smiled. I just nodded and went to put my money away. I wasn't even in the mood to go to this man's section anymore. At least I'll be making money though. I wasn't going to stay in his section long. I was going to drink a little bit, mingle, get some money, and leave.

Once I put my money up, I checked myself in the mirror to make sure I still looked good, then made my way to the flashy nigga's section. When I got up there, he was the only one up there which was weird to me. What was the point of getting a VIP section by yourself? Does he not have friends or something? Once he saw me, his eyes lit up like a kid on Christmas morning.

"I thought you were going to stand a nigga up." he said standing up so that he could hug me. I quickly stepped away from him. I didn't know this nigga and he was trying to hug like we had known each other for years. Nah nigga. Not today we not.

He laughed when I stepped away from him to hide his embarrassment. I could smell the liquor on his breath. I knew he was beyond fucked up, and I was about to take full advantage of that. He picked up a cup and handed it to me. Oh, this nigga must think I'm stupid. I didn't know what the hell he had in that cup. He could've put something in it for all I know. He could be trying to drug my ass.

Just as I took the cup from him, another dancer named Charmaine came into the section too. She had just started working here a couple of weeks ago, and she stayed to herself. I liked her because she wasn't about all the drama like half of the other dancers here. She gave me a weak smile before looking at the cup in my hand.

"Oh shit, I got two beautiful bitches with me. This shit is live." he smiled to himself. I could tell by the look on Charmaine's face that she didn't like the fact that he just called us out our names, but I personally didn't care. I had been called everything in the book. He went to sit down on the couch and Charmaine came closer to me.

"Don't drink that drink. I'm almost certain he put something in it." she said in my ear. I didn't plan on drinking the drink anyway. I appreciated her for looking out for me though. I was wishing she would leave the section so I could do what I planned on doing, but she started making herself really comfortable. She sat down on the couch beside him, and he started kissing all over her neck. Had me fucked up. I wish a nigga would put his crusty ass lips on me.

This nigga grabbed the cup that was on the table and continued to drink. I hope he didn't drive himself here, because I don't know how he was going to make it home alive. That wasn't my problem though. The only thing I was worried about was taking all of this nigga's jewelry and seeing what was in his pockets. I couldn't do that with Charmaine right here, because she was probably going to want in on it, or snitch. Without warning, he passed out, spilling the drink in his hand all over Charmaine.

"What the fuck!" she yelled standing up. She was mad as hell and I couldn't help but smile. "Stupid ass nigga!" she yelled, as she walked out of his section. This was perfect. I quickly walked over to him and snatched all of the chains that were around his neck. I took both Rolexes and went through his pockets to retrieve his wallet. I was feeling like I hit the jackpot right now. This shit was great.

I basically ran out of his section to get back to the locker room. I was ignoring niggas left and right that were trying to grab ahold of me. They probably wanted a dance, but I had other things to worry about right now. I needed to get my shit and leave before this nigga woke up and start wondering where his shit was. I didn't say anything to anyone as I grabbed my duffle bag full of money out of my locker and jetted out of the whole club altogether.

Once I got to my car, I through my duffle bag in the back and got in the driver's seat. I was excited as hell about what I just did. I said I didn't want to rob anyone, but I just couldn't pass this opportunity up. Now it was time to take my ass home, count my money, and go to sleep.

Chapter Eight: Royal

Kaya didn't know this, but I was watching her every move. I was at the club watching her, and she didn't even know it. I know it sounded crazy, but I just needed to make sure she was good. It seemed like she wasn't bothered at all about not talking to me. I was going to give it a couple of days though. After that, if she wants nothing to do with me, then oh well. I can't force her to be with me even though that's what I really wanted.

Watching Kaya dance on stage always had me feeling some type of way. She wasn't supposed to be showing her body to the world like that. That's supposed to be for my eyes only and no one else's. I know… I'm the one who fucked everything up, but she still needed to quit this job. I also saw another side of her today. I watched her run through that nigga's pockets and still his jewelry like it wasn't shit.

First off, he shouldn't be wearing that much jewelry to begin with. He should've known he was bound to get someone's attention with all that shit on, and not the attention he was hoping for either. It was obvious the nigga didn't know how to hold his liquor. Who the hell comes to a strip club alone and gets drunk to the point they pass out? How did this nigga expect to get home? I guess he didn't. Shit, it wasn't my problem at all.

Watching Kaya rob that nigga had my dick hard as hell. I didn't know why, but it did. She knew exactly what she was doing so I know this isn't her first time doing some shit like this. Should I feel some type of way about that? I probably should, but I didn't. There was a lot that I didn't know about Kaya, but that was going to change soon. All I knew was, that nigga is going to be mad as hell when he wakes up and all his shit is gone.

After I watched her pull out of the parking lot, I decided to head home. It was late as hell and I didn't feel like being out anymore. The only reason I was out was to see what Kaya was doing and to make sure she didn't leave with another nigga. Plus, my bed sounded good as hell right now.

Although my bed was calling me, I still ended up in front of Kaya's apartment building. I know I was supposed to be leaving her alone, but I couldn't. She needed to hurry up and forgive me so we could make up and move on from this shit.

Slowly getting out my car, I made my way to her door and just stood there for a minute. I didn't know if I wanted to knock or just take my ass home. I knew she was about to cuss me out, but I really wasn't in the mood for it. I wanted her to let me in, give me something to eat, then let me sleep here for the night. I knew that wasn't going to happen though.

Finally gaining the courage, I lifted my arm and knocked on her door. I stood there for about three minutes before I knocked again. I knew she wasn't sleep yet. Knowing her, she was probably up counting her money and smoking a nasty ass cigarette. That's what she always did when she came home from the club. I heard shuffling, then, finally, the door swung open. Kaya stood there looking like a damn model in her red silk nightgown with her long ass weave falling down to her ass. Sure enough, she had a damn cigarette in her mouth.

"Royal, what the fuck are you doing here?" she asked folding her arms. She looked annoyed, but ask me if I cared. I ignored her little attitude and walked right into the apartment. She had money laid out all over the floor and a bottle of opened wine on her coffee table. I even spotted the wallet and jewelry she stole from ole boy earlier.

"Nigga, I know you hear me. Don't walk up in here like you pay bills and shit." she spat.

"How was work?" I asked sitting down on the couch still ignoring her attitude.

"Get out! Why are you even here? You're not having sex with me, so there's no point for you to be here." She was still smoking her cigarette, and I wanted to knock that shit out of her hand.

"Well I'm here, so get over it." I let her know. She shook her head and stood in front of me with her arms folded. She was looking good enough to eat, but I wasn't even going to try it. I knew she still wasn't fucking with me like that.

"Stupid ass nigga." she mumbled before sitting down on the floor and counting her money. I knew just like she knew that she didn't want me to leave. Otherwise, she would still be running her mouth right now.

I didn't even care that she wasn't talking to me. I was happy just being in her presence. Fuck all that extra shit.

I sat there in silence and watched as she counted her money. I wasn't understanding why she didn't have a money counter. I guess she preferred to do it manually and shit.

"When are you gonna quit that job?" I asked. She cut her eyes at me, then went back to counting her money.

"When are you going to learn how to keep your dick in your pants?" She continued counting her money, but suddenly stopped. "Fuck!" she yelled. She threw the money down and finished off her cigarette. She got up and made her way into the kitchen, then came back with a pack of cigarettes in her hand.

"You need to stop smoking those nasty shits." I let her know. She rolled her eyes at me and lit her cigarette.

"You need to get the hell out my apartment distracting me and shit. If you're gonna be here, stop talking to me. Making me lose count and shit." I smiled at her, which only made her roll her eyes again.

"Nah, I'm not about to do that. I came over here to talk."

"Nigga, talk about what?! You wanna talk about you acting like a little bitch, then cheating on me? Aight my nigga, then talk about it! Talk about how you lost the best thing that's ever happened to you." She was really doing too much right now. All she has to do is hear me out and let me apologize, but she won't even let me do that. This childish shit was starting to piss me off.

"Man, chill with all that yelling shit. I just want to have a conversation like two adults. Or can you not do that because you're too childish?" She chuckled, but she sat her ass down on the couch beside of me

"Talk, nigga." she demanded while blowing out smoke.

"Let me start off by saying I'm sorry for fucking Roxy. I planned on talking to you the next day, but that obviously didn't happen." I said looking down at my hands. I had practiced everything I was going to say to Kaya, but that shit went right out the window. I felt nervous as hell right now.

"Did you use a condom?" she quietly asked like she wasn't sure if she really wanted to know the answer to that or not.

"I always use condoms with these bitches." I said looking directly at her. I probably shouldn't have said it like that because the look on her face let me know that she didn't like what I said at all.

"Dirty dick ass nigga." she scoffed.

"You didn't have to kill the girl." Kaya was acting like she wasn't wrong for what she did. If you ask me, what she did was way worse than what I did. Then she's just sitting here acting like killing bitches is part of her everyday routine.

"I did have to kill her."

"The fuck for?!"

"Because I told her to stay away from my nigga and she didn't listen! I warned the bitch, and she did this shit on purpose!" she yelled standing over me. I smirked at her and stood up. I towered over her little short ass, but she didn't care. She was still standing there like she was about ready to fight my ass.

"You were telling bitches to stay away from me?" I asked.

"Yeah, but I obviously wasted my breath because you still fucked her anyway. This is what I get for trusting a nigga other than Kevin."

"You tryna fuck?"

"What?" I knew she was shocked by my question, but so was I. I wasn't supposed to be giving her dick at all, but she was just looking way too good right now.

"You heard exactly what I said." She looked at me with her face twisted up.

"Nigga, you said you weren't giving me no dick until I was ready to talk to you. Do you not remember saying that shit? It hasn't even been a full twenty-four hours since you said it!" I let out a frustrated breath.

"I know what I said, Kaya. It was a yes or no question. All that other shit is uncalled for." She looked down at her feet like she was afraid to answer the question. She couldn't be, though. Not big bad Kaya.

"Yes." she said barely above a whisper. She almost sounded defeated and that made me smile to myself.

"Yes what?" I asked taking a step closer to her.

"You know what, Royal." she said still not looking up at me.

"Nah, I don't." She sighed and looked up at me.

"I want to fuck you, nigga." She didn't even wait for me to say anything back. She grabbed my hand and took me into her bedroom. Kaya knew she wanted me just as much as I wanted her. She was playing right now. I was going to give her a little minute to herself so she felt like she was doing something, but she was going to be mine again before the end of the month.

After three rounds of straight fucking, Kaya was laid out on the bed staring at the ceiling, while I was trying my hardest to go to sleep. The sun was up, and I was tired as hell. I just needed a quick thirty-minute nap before I left.

"Royal, you need to leave." Kaya quietly said. I should've known that I wasn't going to be able to sleep peacefully while she's still mad at me.

"Give me about thirty minutes." I mumbled.

"No. You need to leave now." I groaned before sitting up in the bed. She had the covers covering her naked body like I'd never saw her naked before. I just shook my head and started putting my clothes back on. She was really doing too much right now. She could've at least let a nigga sleep before putting me out, but that was Kaya for you. Petty as hell. I didn't even say anything to her as I put my shoes on. I felt her staring a hole through me, but I wasn't about to say anything to her. I was pissed off.

"Royal," Kaya said as I walked out of her room. I ignored her and kept walking. She had nothing to say to me right now. Well, if she did, I didn't care. She needed time alone so she could make her mind up about us. That's exactly what I was going to give her too. For real this time.

Walking out of her apartment, I noticed it was pouring down raining. Great. I was tired as hell, it was raining, and looking at the time, I knew the traffic was probably hell right now. That's Atlanta for you. Jogging to my car, I felt my phone ringing in my pocket. I didn't care to answer it, because I was too busy trying not to get too wet. By the time I made it my car, my phone had stopped ringing anyway. I didn't even reach into my pocket to retrieve it. If it was important, they would call back.

As soon as I pulled off, it started ringing again. Who the hell was calling me this early in the first place? Pulling up to a red light, I pulled my phone out of my pocket to see who was calling me. I didn't recognize the number at all, but I decided to just answer it anyway.

"Hello?"

"Royaaaaal." I heard a voice sing. I took the phone away from my ear and looked at it.

"Who the fuck is this, and how the fuck you get my number?" I asked ready to hang up.

"Paisley." I could hear the smile in her voice, but right now, she was the last person that I wanted to be talking to.

"What you want, Paisley?"

"I called to tell you that I'm getting released in a week. Aren't you proud of me?" I chuckled lightly to myself.

"Nah. You shouldn't have been on that shit to begin with. I can't even talk to you without thinking about how you were out there sucking dick for drugs. Shit will never be a good look, ma." I let her know.

"Royal, you need to let that go. I'm leaving that in the past, and so should you. I can't wait to see you next week, though."

"Why would you be seeing me next week?" *Damn, this light is taking forever.* I thought to myself.

"Because you're picking me up. How else would I be getting home?" The light finally turned green, and I sped off.

"Shit, you got a mom right? Why can't she come pick you up? Why I gotta be the one to do the shit?" I really wasn't trying to pick her up from rehab. After I had dropped her off, that's the last time I wanted to deal with her. I couldn't fuck with a bitch that degrades herself for drugs. Nah, shit didn't work like that for me.

"My mom doesn't care about me! I had to beg her to watch my damn daughter… I mean…Umm… Are you coming to get me or not?" I sighed loudly.

"Yeah man. Don't call me until you're actually released." I ended the call and tossed my phone in the passenger's seat. I knew Paisley had friends that she could've called to come get her, but she wants to call me. I also knew that she still wanted a nigga, but I had no interest in her at all anymore. I only had eyes for Kaya who was currently still trippin' right now.

I had been driving for about fifteen minutes with no destination in mind. Kaya not fucking with me was messing my head all up. I needed something that would keep my mind off of her, because I wasn't going to do anything but think about her, then get mad because she put me out this morning. I needed to smoke and maybe even drink. Was it too early for that? I really didn't give a fuck.

I pulled up to Rome's shop, because that nigga always had weed and beer. It was early as hell, but I saw his car in the parking lot. This nigga was here more than he was at home, so I guess him and his girl was still having problems. It seemed like everyone was having women problems.

"Aye, nigga!" I yelled out walking into the building. His receptionist, Brandi, was already here, too, and she looked at me and rolled her eyes. I smiled at her and kept it moving. Rome was sitting in his office chair with a blunt dangling from his lips while he scrolled through his phone.

"You here early as shit." he said not even looking up at me.

"Yeah, Kaya kicked me out her apartment. I barely got any sleep."

"Damn. She's still not fucking with you?"

"Man, hell nah. Shit starting to piss me off." I sat down on the couch and blew out a frustrated breath.

"Give her time, nigga. You forcing yourself on her is only gonna make her hate your ass even more." He put his phone down and started rolling up another blunt. He had one in his mouth, but here he was rolling up another one. Nigga must be stressing.

"I don't want to give her ass time. Shit, I fucked up, she killed the bitch, I apologized. Why can't we move on from this shit?" Rome started laughing like I had told the world's funniest joke or some shit.

"You hurt her feelings nigga! She's not just going to forget that shit. Then it just happened. You didn't even give her a month to get over it." He shook his head at me.

"Did you give Clay a month to get over it?"

"Hell no. She tried to move in with her mom and shit, but I wasn't having that. She could be mad all she wanted, but she was going to be in the house that we shared. Fuck that." He shrugged his shoulders like what he was saying was okay. I wasn't going to force Kaya to live with me and shit, because I knew her ass wouldn't do that. She would probably try to kill my ass if I even tried to do some shit like that. I gotta be careful around her, knowing that she's crazy and went around slitting throats like it's an everyday activity or some shit.

"I can't do that with Kaya. She's crazy."

"Yeah, she'll probably try to kill your ass. That's why you just gotta give her some time. Let her come to you." I looked at this nigga like he was crazy.

"That ain't gonna happen. I'm better off being single and doing what I was doing before I met Kaya."

"Then do it, nigga. She obviously has feelings for yo' ass because she's killing bitches over you and shit. She'll be back. I can promise that." I thought about what Rome said and decided to do just that. I could have fun right now, because I'm single, right?

Chapter Nine: Clay

I knew Rome wanted me to stay in the house, but that wasn't about to work. It had been about two weeks and that Nikki bitch was still living. If you ask me, he should be the one to kill her, but who knows what goes on in that stupid little head of his. It was obvious that, if I wanted results, I would have to do the shit myself.

Kaya and Erica were already at my house waiting for me to finish getting dressed. Kaya told me that I should wear all black, but it was day time. What was the point of that? It wasn't like we were going to rob someone. I just wanted to get in and get out. Simple.

When I walked down the stairs, Kaya and Erica were staring at each other like they were ready for war. I knew it probably wasn't the greatest idea to have those two in the same room, but I felt like I needed the both of them for what I was about to do. Kaya, of course, was wearing an all-black bodysuit and was smoking a cigarette. I rolled my eyes at her.

"Kaya, put that shit out." I snapped.

"I told her that you didn't like when people smoked in the house, but she didn't listen to me." Erica said.

"Bitch, shut the fuck up. You didn't tell me shit." Kaya put her cigarette out in the ashtray that was on the coffee table, then stood up. "I'm ready to get this over with. I might end up killing this bitch if I'm around her for too long." she said walking out the house. I looked at Erica who just rolled her eyes. She was afraid of Kaya. It was written all over her face.

"Why did you even invite her?" Erica had the nerve to ask. I didn't even answer that stupid ass question. I just walked out of the house right behind Kaya. It was something bothering her other than Erica.

"What's the matter?" I asked getting in the driver's seat of my car.

"Nothing." she muttered scrolling through her phone.

"Girl, don't start this shit. What the hell is wrong with you?" She looked at me and sighed.

"I haven't heard from Royal in two weeks." I looked at her with a raised eyebrow.

"Why would you want to hear from him? Aren't you done with him?"

"Yes… No… I don't know. I don't know how to feel, really." Erica got in the backseat, and I already knew that Kaya wasn't going to talk about Royal anymore. Erica would be happy to know that Royal wasn't fucking with Kaya like that anymore.

"So where does this bitch live?" Erica asked.

"Right beside of my mom." Just thinking about Nikki made my blood boil. All this time she lived right beside my mom, and I didn't even know it. I could've been gotten rid of her ass.

"Damn, for real? That's crazy. How are we gonna get her to come outside though? We're not just going to walk in her house are we? What if the door is locked? Did y'all really think this plan through? It's not seeming like it."

"Damn Erica, shut the fuck up for once. You talk too damn much! Clay, why the fuck did you tell this bitch to come anyway?" Kaya spat. I pulled up to a red light and tried my hardest not to laugh. Kaya was always snapping on Erica, and Erica would never say anything.

"Because she wanted me to come, obviously. You always talking shit." Erica finally grew some balls and said.

"Bitch—" Kaya started but didn't finish. She quickly undid her seatbelt and opened the door.

"Kaya! What the hell are you doing?!" I shrieked. She was acting like we weren't in the middle of traffic. She ran over to Erica's side of the car and pulled the door open.

"Bitch, I owe you an ass whoopin' anyway!" Kaya yelled while dragging Erica out the car by her hair. Once she had Erica on the ground, it was over. Kaya was really beating her ass in the middle of traffic. Cars were honking at us and getting mad, but I couldn't pay attention to that. My main focus was getting Kaya's crazy ass back in the damn car.

"Kaya!" I yelled once I was out the car. Erica wasn't even fighting back. This bitch was balled up trying to protect her face as Kaya kicked her all over her body. This is some straight ratchet shit man. I wanted to pull Kaya off of Erica, but I didn't want to risk getting hit in my stomach. Kaya looked like a mad woman right now. I almost felt bad for Erica.

"You're the reason Royal cheated on me, stupid bitch!" Kaya yelled while still hitting her. She had her knee on Erica's chest so she couldn't go anywhere. She was delivering punch after punch, and Erica wasn't even fighting back. This wasn't even a fight.

"You should've kept your damn mouth shut! I should kill your ass right now." Kaya continued to scream while hitting her. I was starting to regret that I even brought Erica with us. This was not supposed to happen. At least, not today. She should've saved it for another day.

I guess Kaya finally got tired of hitting Erica and Erica not fighting back because she calmly got off of her and got back in the car like nothing happened. Yeah, my friend was definitely crazy. There was no doubt about that.

"UGH! I NEED A FUCKING CIGARETTE!" she yelled. I helped Erica off the ground, and her face was all fucked up. Her lip was busted and her nose was bleeding. She had a cut right above her eyebrow that was also bleeding, and I'm sure in a couple of hours, one of her eyes would be swollen.

"Why didn't you help me?" Erica asked snatching away from me. She just got her ass beat by Kaya, and she had the nerve to be mad at me? What kind of shit is that?

"Don't be mad at me because you can't fight, Erica. Get in the damn car so we can go." I shook my head and got back in the driver's seat. Kaya was sitting in the front seat looking evil as hell. I still wanted to laugh, but I decided against it. That would probably make things a lot worse.

"Stupid ass bitch." Kaya said to herself. Erica just sat in the backseat pouting like a big ass baby. I chuckled and drove off. There was never a dull moment when I was with Kaya. I just wished her and Royal could get it together so she could be happy again. I don't like seeing her sad and shit. That's not something that usually happens, because Kaya never was sad over a nigga.

The whole ride to Nikki's house was a quiet one, other than hearing Erica sniffle occasionally. This was the most awkward car ride ever. I didn't know what the hell she was crying for. She should've just learned to keep her mouth shut. She shouldn't have even said anything to Royal about her fucking niggas for money. That was petty as hell, and to be honest, I feel like Erica deserved that beat down.

"That's the house right there." I told Kaya and Erica. I pulled into my mom's driveway, because I didn't want to attract unwanted attention to us.

"How are we gonna get in this damn house?" Erica pressed. She obviously didn't know what Kaya was capable of. Kaya and I didn't bother replying to Erica. We both just simply got out the car and made our way to Nikki's front door.

"Are y'all seriously about to knock?" Erica asked. I turned and looked at her. The blood was starting to dry on her face, and she looked terrible.

"Erica, shut the fuck up. That's all you need to do right now." I let her know. We all stood quietly as Kaya picked the lock. I'll never understand how she knows how to do that, but I was glad she did. This shit really came in handy.

Once the door was open, we all stepped into the house. It was quiet as hell, and the shit made me feel a little nervous.

"Get behind me." Kaya whispered like she was the man of the group or something. Erica and I didn't hesitate to get behind her, either. She was the only one who had a gun. She was the only one who knew how to use a gun, too.

Following behind Kaya, quietly, my nerves started messing with me. I was now starting to think that what we were doing wasn't a good idea at all. I've never killed anyone before, but Kaya has. That's why she was so excited to come with me. I don't know what I'm going to do if I see a dead body. That's not something you see every day. It's just not right.

Walking into the master bedroom, I was relieved to see that no one was in there. I let out a sigh of relief as Kaya looked around. She looked aggravated as hell.

"There's no one in this damn house." Kaya said.

"This was a waste of time." Erica mumbled to herself.

"You shouldn't even be here. You ain't about that life." Kaya spat.

"Hey, both of y'all shut the hell up. I don't want to hear this shit." I said. They were starting to get on my nerves. I understood that they didn't like each other, but damn. Just shut the hell up.

"Clay, what do you want to do now?" Kaya asked looking around the room, which was actually really clean. Nikki must've been a neat freak or something.

"I guess we can just leave. I'll catch her some other time." I said as I started to walk out.

"No. Let's fuck this shit up so she knows that someone has been in her house." I looked at Kaya like she was crazy. Wait, no… Kaya was crazy. She doesn't think things through at all. I guess consequences doesn't scare her at all.

"No! We'll get her another time." I said. She ignored me as she started messing the room up. She was taking clothes out of the closet and throwing them on the floor. She took the covers off the bed, threw the TV on the floor causing it to break, and even took the girl's makeup and threw it everywhere. Kaya looked like she was having the time of her life right now. You would think she was the one that Nikki was messing with and not me.

"Clay, go find some bleach or something." Kaya said.

"What? Why?" I looked at Erica, who was looking scared as hell. I didn't know why I told her to come with us. Kaya was right. She wasn't about that life at all.

"Just go do it! You have the opportunity to fuck up the girl's house who yo' nigga cheated on you with, and you're just gonna stand there and look stupid?" She had a point. I should be doing everything that Kaya was doing right now, and enjoying it.

I walked out the room and went to go look for the bleach and whatever else I could find. I found the bleach in the laundry room, and I went into the kitchen to see if she had mustard that I could squirt on everything. I found the mustard, but I decided to fuck up the kitchen before I went back into her room.

Taking everything out of the refrigerator, I threw food all over the floor. I went to the cabinets and threw every glass dish she had on the floor too. By the time I was finished, food was everywhere, broken glass was everywhere, and it looked like a tornado had hit her kitchen. I went and found a knife and made my way into her living room. I smiled to myself as I cut up all of her couches. They were all leather and looked like they cost a lot of money, but I didn't give a fuck. This was actually pretty fun.

"Stupid bitch." I muttered to myself as I went to the plants that she had all over the place. I picked every plant up and poured them out onto the carpet. Soil and water went everywhere. This was just too great.

She had a flat screen TV sitting on the TV stand, and I pushed that shit right to the floor. I laughed as I looked around the living room and kitchen and saw the damage that I had caused. I grabbed the bleach and walked back into the bedroom. Erica was standing in the corner looking scared as Kaya was still throwing clothes and shit around.

"This bitch left the house without her wallet." Kaya laughed while holding the wallet in her hand. I just shook my head because this girl was really stupid.

"I got the bleach." I said holding up the two jugs of bleach that I had in my hands.

"Wonderful." Kaya smiled as she grabbed one. She opened it and started pouring it all over her clothes and the bed. She even threw some of it on the walls, so I started doing the same thing. I hope Nikki knows I'm the one who did this to her house. Maybe I should leave a note or something.

"Did y'all hear that?" Erica asked looking paranoid as hell. I rolled my eyes at her scary ass.

"Girl shut up. There ain't nothing out there." Kaya said. We continued messing up her room until we heard a loud, piercing scream.

"What the hell are y'all doing?! How did y'all even get in my house?!" Nikki yelled. I turned around to see her standing at the door of her room with her mouth hanging open.

"What the fuck are you yelling about?" another voice said. A voice that I knew all too well. A voice that had no damn business being here… Rome. He came and stood behind Nikki, but he froze when he saw me. I felt like my heart had just been kicked in the ass. What the hell was he even doing here? Why was he with her right now when he was supposed to be at work? Why was he still communicating with her after the crazy bitch tried to kill me? I couldn't deal with this. I was too done with him.

"Clay—" He started, but I cut him off.

"Don't even bother. It's obvious she's the one you want, so I'm gonna let y'all two live happily ever after." I said as I slid the ring off my finger and handed it to Nikki. She took it like a dumb ass and was admiring it like Rome had actually bought it for her.

"Clay, it's not what it looks like. I don't want this girl." he said trying to grab my arm, but I snatched away from him.

"You don't want me? Then, why you keep texting me telling me you can't wait to see me again and shit? Don't try to front because your little girlfriend is standing right here." Nikki said. I'd heard enough, and I was done. I wasted my time coming here and destroying her things, because my nigga was still entertaining her. It's funny how he was playing both sides.

"Y'all, let's go." I said feeling the tears build up. I was not about to cry in front of them, though. I wasn't going to give them the satisfaction of seeing me cry.

"Niggas ain't shit." Kaya said. Nikki scoffed and rolled her eyes. I guess Kaya didn't like that Nikki rolled her eyes, because she threw the empty bleach container at her, and it hit her in the face. I just walked out of the house. This shit was pointless now. I wasn't shocked that Rome didn't bother to follow me. It was obvious that he cared about Nikki more than he cared about me.

I walked to my car by myself, but I still didn't let the tears fall. I shouldn't be crying because he fucked up. He should be crying because he just lost the best thing that's ever happened to him. Kaya and Erica came out the house, as I got in the car and started it. I needed to leave. I didn't want to be around Rome ever again. I didn't want to go live with my mom either. I guess it was time to look for an apartment now.

"Are you gonna be okay?" Kaya asked when she got in the car. I just nodded my head and drove off. I didn't feel like talking right now. I didn't feel like doing anything but packing my shit and leaving this no good ass nigga. I was done looking dumb over him. It wasn't even worth it anymore.

Chapter Ten: Rome

I know this looks bad, but it's not what you think at all. The only reason I'm even around Nikki right now is because I planned on ending her life today. I knew I could easily do it by coming to her crib, but the last person I expected to be here was Clay. I already know that she's not going to listen to anything that I have to say.

"Look what they did to my house!" Nikki yelled. Her house was fucked up. I couldn't believe they were actually in here messing her house up. I just wanted to know how the hell they got in here in the first place. This had Kaya's name written all over it. Kaya was the only one who would do some crazy shit like this.

"I'm gonna kill that bitch." Nikki mumbled, as she tried to clean up the mess they made. There was no cleaning it up though. She picked up her clothes, which now had bleach all over them. The bleach smell was strong as hell and was making me sick. I needed to get out of here before I passed out.

Nikki walked out the room and into the living room. She started screaming, so I slowly made my way out the bedroom to see what her crazy ass was screaming about now. There was soil all over the carpet, and food was all over the floor in the kitchen. I would be mad as hell if I was Nikki, but I didn't feel bad for her at all.

"How could you let her do this to my house? Y'all planned this out didn't y'all?" She asked looking at me with nothing but hate in her eyes.

"What? You talkin' crazy, girl." I said with a light chuckle.

"No I'm not! You knew she was going to do this! How the hell did they even get in my house?! I know you had something to do with this Rome! I should call the police and have your stupid girlfriend arrested for breaking and entering! They fucked up my whole wardrobe! That shit is expensive!" she yelled. I ignored her because I knew she wasn't going to do shit. She was just a shit talker.

"I ain't have shit to do with it." I said, nonchalantly. She picked up a glass flower pot that was on the floor and threw it at my head barely missing it. Now this bitch was trippin'.

"The fuck is wrong with you?!" I yelled getting in her face.

"Nothing is wrong with me. You're the one with the problem. You really had that girl come in here and fuck up my house." She folded her arms and shook her head. I needed to do what I came here to do and get the fuck out of here. I already knew that Clay was probably at the house packing up her things as we speak. I didn't even know why I was still here in the first place.

Pulling out my gun, I aimed it directly at her head. Her eyes grew wide, and she opened her mouth to say something but quickly closed it.

"I regret the day I met your stupid ass. You really thought that you could attack my pregnant fiancé and I would just let yo' ass get away with it? You got me fucked up, bruh." I said through gritted teeth.

"Rome, I—" I cut her words short by pressing my gun harder into her temple.

"Shut the fuck up. I don't give a fuck what you got to say right now. Ever since you decided you wanted to come back into my life, you've fucked up a lot of shit between me and my girl. Now I gotta go beg for her to take me back because of you."

"I just wanted you to love me as much as you love her! I can be the side hoe. I won't say anything, I promise." The fact that Nikki was actually serious about being a side now had me ready to laugh in her face, but right now, this was a serious moment.

"Nah." I said looking directly into her eyes. Of course she started crying like she always did when I tell her I don't want her. You would think she's crying about her life flashing right before her eyes, but no. She's crying because I'm in a relationship and will never love her.

"Nikki!" I heard a voice call out. Shit. I quickly put my gun away and stepped away from Nikki. The same girl that was with Nikki at the hospital came into the living room with a disgusted look on her face.

"Nikki, what the hell happened to your house?" she asked. She was wearing a sports bra and leggings, looking like she had just come from the gym. I had to admit, her body was a work of art. Her dark skin made it look even better. I had to force myself to look away from her.

"He got his girlfriend to mess my house up!" Nikki yelled through her tears.

"Yo, stop saying that shit. I didn't get her to do shit, bruh." I spat.

"Um, is this a bad time? Should I come back later?"

"Nah, I'm out." I said making my way to the door. Every time I tried to kill this delusional bitch, something always happened. The next time I'm not going to do any talking. I'm just going to kill her ass and be on my way.

I got to my car, and the first thing I did was call Clay. It didn't surprise me when sent me straight to voicemail. Knowing her, she either blocked me, or turned her phone off. I didn't give a fuck though. I wasn't about to let Clay leave me. Especially, when I wasn't doing anything wrong.

As I was breaking every traffic law to make it home to Clay, I was starting to regret not killing Nikki once again. I felt like it was only going to get worse from here. Nikki was the type of person that doesn't know when to stop, and I already know she's going to keep messing with Clay until I end her life. I plan on ending her life the very next time I see her. I just had to make sure I didn't waste any time by talking too damn much.

"Fuck." I said to myself as I stopped at a red light. I didn't even know how I was going to explain myself to Clay, because I knew she wasn't going to care about anything that I had to say to her right now. I guess I could give her some space and let her calm down, but fuck that. She needed to talk to me right now, not later. That's that childish shit.

Happy was an understatement when I pulled up to my house and saw Clay's car in the driveway. Maybe she realized she was trippin' earlier and she decided to stay. I sure hoped that was what it was. I quickly got out my car and ran into the house. My clothes weren't thrown all over the place like I expected them to be, and it was quiet as hell in the house.

I ran up the stairs to find Clay sitting on the bed eating ice cream out of the box and watching TV like everything was okay. She didn't even look at me as I stood beside the bed. She just kept eating her ice cream like I wasn't even there.

"Clay, we need to talk." I said sitting down on the bed beside her. She still didn't look at me, but she chuckled.

"No we don't." she calmly said. I wasn't feeling this shit at all. I was used to Clay flipping the fuck out on me, not this calm shit. I would feel a lot better if she was throwing things at me, cussing me out or even destroying my clothes.

"Yes we do. I was only at Nikki's house for one reason."

"And what reason was that? So you could get your dick sucked? If you wanted to be with her, that's all you had to say. I would've let you two live happily ever after, and I damn sure wouldn't be pregnant by you right now." I let out a frustrated breath.

"Clay, shut the fuck up and listen. I was only over there so I could kill her bitch ass. I was going to make it quick, then be on my way. I didn't expect you to be there destroying her house and shit."

"Did you kill her?"

"Nah." She finally looked at me and rolled her eyes.

"Why didn't you kill her this time, Rome? Because she told you how much she loves you? What's your excuse now?"

"Because somebody walked into the fuckin' house."

"Then you should've killed them too!" Kaya was definitely rubbing off on her, because Clay wasn't this type of person. She hated when innocent people got killed for no reason, but now she's sitting here telling me I should've killed a girl who had nothing to do with what Nikki did.

"So, you're telling me that I should've killed an innocent person?" I asked. She averted her attention back to the TV and didn't say anything. She knew just like I knew that the girl didn't deserve to lose her life over Nikki's crazy ass.

"You keep making me look stupid." she said quietly.

"Fuck you talkin' about?"

"How would you feel if you went to some nigga's house to kill him, and I showed up with that nigga? You know how embarrassing that was for me? I'm there to get rid of her so we can have a healthy relationship again, and you want to be sneaking around with the bitch."

"I wasn't sneaking around with the bitch." I defended.

"Yes the hell you were! You couldn't have told me what you had planned? Shit, we could've done it together!" She had a point, but I didn't want her to do anything crazy while she was pregnant.

"You're pregnant, and you all you need to do is sit back and let ya man handle shit."

"You're not my man." she said looking at me again.

"I'm not?" I smirked, while taking the ice cream container out of her hands and lying her down on the bed.

"Nope." She breathed. I kissed her on her neck causing her body to tremble like I knew it would. She was only talking shit so she could get the dick. She did it all the time. I think she likes makeup sex better than regular sex. That's why she's always acting like she's mad at me and shit.

"You sure about that?" I asked slipping my hand in the shorts she had on.

"I'm positive." she said. I start nibbling on her neck while slipping two fingers inside of her.

"How positive are you?"

"Rome," she moaned while throwing her head back.

"Answer my question, Clay." I said moving so that our lips were inches from touching.

"I'm… Shit." she whispered.

"You're what?"

"One hundred…percent…Romeee." I licked her bottom lip before pulling my fingers out of her. Her head shot up and she looked at me with the ugliest expression. "What the fuck?" she folded her arms, and I just smiled lying down on the bed beside her.

"I'm not your man, right? I'm not making you cum since I'm not your man."

"Are you serious? Nigga, you play too damn much." she spat getting off the bed and storming into the bathroom. She slammed the door, and I couldn't help but smile. She was really in there pouting like a big baby, but it was her own fault. She knows she's not going anywhere. I don't know why she's always acting like she is.

A few moments later, I heard the shower turn on, and I decided that I was going to join her. That was until my phone rang, letting me know that I had a text message. Picking up my phone, I saw that the number that was texting me wasn't saved. I wasn't even going to bother opening the message, but a picture popped up.

I unlocked my phone and went to the picture. Imagine my surprise to see that someone had sent me a picture of their breasts. I hurried and deleted the picture. Maybe they just had the wrong number or something. If Clay was to see that, she would leave my ass for sure. I couldn't have that shit. Clay was stuck with me for the rest of her life, especially since she was now carrying my baby.

I sat up in the bed, about to take off my clothes so I could join her in the shower, but my phone started ringing again. This time, I was getting a phone call from the number that just texted me. Should I even answer this? It's obvious they have the wrong number. I guess the least I could do was let them know they had the wrong number and to stop sending me those kinds of pictures.

"Hello?" I said answering the phone.

"Did you get my picture, Rome?" a voice asked. I pulled the phone from my ear and looked at it as if I could see the caller on the other end of it.

"Yo, who the fuck is this?" I asked already feeling myself getting mad.

"Don't act like you don't know." The voice sounded familiar as hell, but I was hoping it wasn't who I thought it was.

"I don't."

"I think you do. Is that daughter of mine around? Is that why you're acting like you don't know who I am? It has to be."

"Tracy? Man, how the fuck you get my number, bruh?" Tracy really wasn't shit. What kind of mother tries to fuck her own daughter's boyfriend? She doesn't even care about Clay's feelings.

"Don't worry about how I got your number. When are you going to leave her so we can be together? Don't let my age scare you away." she had the nerve to say. I was at a loss for words right now. How could people be so damn grimy? I heard the shower in the bathroom cut off, and I knew Clay would be out here soon, because she didn't like drying off in the bathroom.

"Aye man, lose my number. Don't call or text me ever again, or I'm gonna let your daughter know what you're trying to do." I said. I hung up before she could even respond. As soon as I was done blocking her number, Clay walked out the bathroom in nothing but her towel looking like a walking goddess.

"Why didn't you come join me in the shower?" she pouted. I chuckled. The only reason she went to take a shower was so I could join her and fuck the shit out of her in the process.

"My bad. You seemed mad, so I thought I would give you your space." I lied hoping she didn't see through my lies like she always did.

"Are you going to give me some dick or not? I'm tired of playing these games with you." I smiled and got off the bed, making my way over to her. Everything her mom had just said to me went out the window as soon as her towel hit the floor. Ever since Clay found out that she was pregnant, her sex drive has been higher than mine. She's always trying to out fuck me, but I ain't letting that shit happen.

"Rome, if I find out you're texting other bitches, I'm killing you and her." Clay moaned as she rode my dick. She had her eyes closed, with her head thrown all the way back, and her mouth was hanging open. She had me about to cum just from looking at her. I was one stupid ass nigga for cheating on her. Especially for cheating on her with a bitch like Nikki. Nikki didn't have shit on Clay. Even on her worst day.

"Damn, girl." I mumbled. Her titties were bouncing all over the place, and I wanted to put them in my mouth, but I knew that wasn't about to happen because I felt my but building up. "Slow down, Ma." I told her. She opened her eyes and looked at me, then started smirking.

"Slow down? Nah." she said smiling. She put both of her hands on my chest and start riding me even harder. She was playing too much right now and making my toes curl in the process. Her moans quickly turned into screams as she held onto one of her breasts. I just closed my eyes. She knew exactly what she was doing; that's the only reason she wanted to get on top. So she could dominate me and feel like she was in control.

I bit down hard on my bottom lip feeling myself about to cum, and Clay got off of me. She laid down on the bed breathing hard while I was looking at her like she had lost her damn mind.

"What the fuck, Clay?" I damn near shouted.

"Now you see how it feels when you're about to cum, but the person just stops. I'm good though. I got mine." she smiled.

"Clay, don't play with me. Finish what the hell you started."

"No, I'm good. I'm actually kinda tired. I think I'm gonna take a little nap now." She turned her back towards me, and I just laid there fuming with a hard dick. It was okay though. I had something for her ass since she wanted to be childish and shit.

"Childish as fuck." I said to myself as I got up to go to the bathroom. Two could play this game, only I could play it better.

Chapter Eleven: Reese

It had been about a week since I went to Nikki's house and found it in shambles. She claimed that Rome's girlfriend was the one that did it, but I didn't believe that at all. I honestly didn't know what to believe when it came to Nikki now. She was proving herself to be really crazy over a man that wants nothing to do with her. I keep telling her to leave Rome alone and let him be happy in his relationship, but she didn't listen. She keeps trying to come up with ways to break them up, and I keep telling her that it's not going to happen. I'm starting to sound like a broken record over here.

"You always have something negative to say about Rome and I. That's probably why you and Kevin aren't together anymore. Because you're just a negative person and no one wants to deal with that." Nikki told me. She had been staying with me while she got someone to clean her house up. I didn't understand why she couldn't just clean it up herself. I was starting to wish she did, because she was starting to get annoying. All she did was talk about Rome, and she kept throwing the fact that I was no longer with Kevin in my face.

"Everything I say about you and Rome is the truth." I said walking into the kitchen to retrieve my ringing cell phone. I looked to see who was calling and rolled my eyes. Kevin makes it his business to call me at least five times a day. I've already told him that I want nothing to do with him. Whatever we had is over. Why would I want to be with someone who couldn't keep their dick in their pants? I hit ignore on my phone, then put it on silent, because I knew he was going to call right back.

"You don't know what you're talking about. That man loves me just as much as I love him. He just puts on a front when other people are around." I didn't respond to her, because I was too busy watching my phone light up again with a call from Kevin. I wanted so badly to answer it. I wanted to hear his voice, and most of all, I wanted things to go back to how they used to be between us. He just had to go and mess things up.

"Hello?" I answered without thinking about what I was doing.

"Reeseee." Kevin slurred into the phone. He was obviously drunk right now. This didn't shock me.

"What do you want, Kevin."

"I want you, girl. You're the girl of my dreamsss." he sang. I couldn't help but blush. This nigga wasn't shit, and I knew that, but here I was blushing at what he had just sang to me.

"I'm obviously not. Your baby's mother is the girl of your dreams." I spat angrily.

"Fuck that bitch, man! I want you! I want to fuck you! I'm putting a ring on your finger!" I didn't say anything back, because I honestly didn't know what to say. Kevin was drunk right now, and he probably didn't know what he was saying. Did he? "You hear me? Let me come over so we can talk this out."

"No. We don't have anything to talk about. Plus, you don't need to be driving while you're drunk." I hated that I cared so much about this man. He broke my heart, and I was still worried about his well-being. Ugh.

"Fuck all that. I'm good to drive. Shit." I heard a lot of shuffling on his end of the phone.

"Kevin, I'm serious. Put your damn keys down and go to sleep. We don't have anything to talk about." I said in a stern voice.

"But I need to see you, baby." This conversation was making me weak. It was making me want to kick Nikki out and go pick Kevin up from where ever he was at, because I was not going to let him drive around while he was drunk.

"Kevin…" I closed my eyes to fight back the tears that were threatening to fall. I knew I shouldn't have answered his phone call. He has a way of making me weak, and he doesn't even have to be in my presence.

"I'm on the way." he said then ended the call. Shit. I immediately called him back, but he didn't answer. I tried four more times before I eventually just gave up. There was no stopping him from drunk driving. I just prayed that he made it here safely. I might lose my mind if something happens to him tonight.

"Should've never answered." I said out loud.

"What? What are you talking about?" Nikki asked. For a moment, I forgot that she was even here.

"Nothing." I said walking into my bedroom. My nerves were all over the place right now.

"Who called? Was it Kevin? Are y'all getting back together?" Nikki asked following right behind me.

"Girl, mind your business." I looked down at my phone to see if Kevin had called back, but unfortunately, he hadn't.

"I just asked a simple question. There's no need to catch an attitude." she said with a roll of her eyes. Right now, I just wanted Nikki to go away. I was about to go crazy not knowing what Kevin was doing right now. I sat down on the bed and took a deep breath. Maybe he would fall asleep before he left his house and wouldn't make it over here. Just maybe. Why wasn't he answering his phone though? I know he saw me calling him.

About twenty minutes had passed and I still hadn't heard anything from Kevin. I felt like my heart was going to beat right out of my chest, I was so nervous. Nervous because I didn't want him to get in a car accident, and because I hadn't seen him in a while. I didn't know how this was about to go.

"So are you going to tell me what's bothering you now? You've been sitting here looking nervous for about twenty minutes now." Nikki said looking at me with a concerned look.

"I'm good." I said quickly getting off the bed and slipping my bedroom shoes on.

"Then where are you going?"

"I'll be right back." I said making my way out of the apartment. I walked down the stairs just to see if I could spot Kevin's car. I didn't want him to see me, because I didn't want him to think that I was overly eager, even though I was.

As soon as I got downstairs, I knew exactly which car was his. He was doubled parked, and the music was blasting. The only thing was, it looked like he was passed out in the front seat. I could hardly tell, though, because the tint on his windows was so damn obscure. I deliberately made my way to the car to make sure he was alright. I knew I should probably just leave him where he was and go on with my life, but I couldn't. I missed him, and I still cared about his ass.

I sighed once I was at his door. He sure enough was passed out in the driver's seat with a bottle of beer in his hand that spilled all over his shirt. He looked so pathetic right now, but he was still so dang good looking. Mouth hanging open and all, he was still something to look at. I wish he wasn't. Maybe then, I could leave him right in the car and not care about if he made it home safely.

After about five minutes of just gazing at him, I finally decided that I was going to try to get him out the car and take him upstairs to my apartment. At least so he could sober up a bit. Oh, who was I kidding? He was going to stay at my apartment all night, because I refused to let him drive anywhere else tonight.

Turning the car off, and taking the keys out of the ignition, I regrettably pulled Kevin out the car. I didn't expect him to be so heavy. It felt like this man weighed as much as his damn car.

"Goodness gracious." I said as I tried to get him to stand up. I was beyond grateful when he woke up.

"Reese," he said barely above a whisper. "I'm tryna fuck tonight." I'm not even going to lie and pretend like the thought of us having sex tonight didn't thrill me. I knew I wasn't going to do it though. He was only going to be here until the morning, then I was going to send him on his way. I didn't want him thinking that he had a chance of getting back with me just because I was letting him stay in my apartment for the night.

"No." I harshly said struggling to get him up the stairs. This, by far, had to be one of the toughest things I think I've ever done. He was so heavy, it didn't make any sense.

"I'm getting in them guts tonight!" he yelled. I was so glad no one was outside, because this would've been highly embarrassing.

"Kevin, be quiet. It's late, and people are trying to sleep."

"I'm trying to sleep with you, girl." He started laughing, and I rolled my eyes. He probably won't remember any of this tomorrow morning.

When we finally made it to the top of the stairs, I wanted to shout for joy. My happiness was short-lived when I saw Jay standing at his door smoking a cigarette and talking on the phone. He was looking better than Kevin was right now in his all-black shirt and skinny jeans that weren't too tight. His hair, as always, was up in that sexy ass man bun that he did, and his tattoos were on full display. Goodness, he was so good looking.

He looked at me and smirked, but I quickly looked away from him. I wasn't really his biggest fan. He was rude as hell, and I had to keep reminding myself that.

"Who the hell is this nigga, and why is he smiling so hard at you?" Kevin asked trying to stand all the way up. This is another thing that I wanted to avoid. Kevin was a damn hot head, and his temper was terrible. He would fight anyone and worry about the consequences later.

"Be quiet, Kevin." I whispered to him.

"Nah, I ain't gotta be quiet. I wanna know who this nigga is and why he thinks it's okay to be staring at you so hard. You know this nigga?" Kevin was still talking loud, and now Jay was making his way toward us with the ugliest expression on his face. This wasn't going to end well at all. I could feel it.

"You got a problem, man?" Jay asked Kevin. Kevin slightly pushed me off of him and stood as if he were ready to fight. He knew he shouldn't be fighting while he was drunk like this.

"Hell yeah, nigga! Why the fuck you staring at my girl like that? She don't want you, nigga! Keep your eyes to yourself!" Kevin bellowed.

"Kevin! Be quiet!" I shrieked.

"This ya mans?" Jay asked with a light laugh.

"No, he's my ex. We're not together anymore. He drove over here drunk, and I'm not about to let him drive home while he is drunk." I explained. I didn't know what made me explain myself to Jay. He wasn't my type, and I damn sure wasn't trying to be in a relationship with him. He nodded his head and started walking towards his apartment. He ignored everything Kevin was yelling, and I was glad.

"Kevin, shut the hell up!" I snapped. I opened the door to my apartment and pushed him in. Of course he had to be dramatic and fall on the floor like I pushed him extra hard or something. I rolled my eyes and stepped over him.

"Damn Reese, why you do a nigga like that?" he asked trying to pull himself up. Nikki, who was sitting on the couch, was looking at me with a raised eyebrow. I ignored her look and helped Kevin off the floor.

"What's he doing here?" she asked.

"Be quiet, Nikki." Kevin and I struggled to get to my room, and when we finally did, he collapsed on the bed.

"Reeseee," he groaned with his face in the pillow. "Come lay with me." I was irritated right now, and I wish he would've never brought his drunk ass over here. I don't have time to be babysitting a grown ass man. I wasn't about to sleep in the living room with Nikki though. I didn't want to hear her mouth, and I didn't feel like talking about why Kevin was here right now. I was honestly wishing she wasn't even here. She didn't know how to mind her business, and it was annoying as hell.

I heard light snores coming from Kevin, and I was a little relieved. He needed to be sleeping so he would stop talking to me. I was almost certain that he was going to have the worst hangover in the morning. That wasn't my problem though. The only thing he needed to do tomorrow morning was find his way out of my apartment and take his ass home.

I cut out the light, then slid in bed beside Kevin. I missed sleeping beside him and cuddling with him at night. He smelled like beer mixed with whatever cologne he had on, and it wasn't a pleasant smell at all. I didn't want to take his clothes off, but I couldn't deal with this smell. Hell no. Not in my bed.

Getting out of bed, I tried my hardest to turn him over on his back. I still couldn't believe how heavy he was. All I wanted to do was take off his shirt. I was going to leave his pants on, because I honestly didn't trust myself right now. Finally getting him on his back, I removed his shirt and admired all of the tattoos that were all over his chest. I balled the shirt up and threw it in the corner of my room. I knew he was going to be mad about that in the morning, because he hated when his clothes were on the floor, but I honestly didn't care.

I went to the edge of the bed so I could try to remove his shoes too. I didn't want his nasty ass shoes on my clean sheets. I had just changed them, and he was not about to dirty them up. Not on my watch. Once his shoes were off, I went back to my side of the bed and tried to get some sleep. Unfortunately, sleep didn't come easy for me at all. I laid in bed for hours just listening to Kevin snore. I didn't expect him to be in my bed again, and I damn sure didn't expect to be in this situation with him. I just needed the morning to hurry up and get here.

***

"Fuck." I heard Kevin's deep voice mumble. I felt movement, which was probably him getting off the bed. I kept my eyes closed, because I wasn't quite ready to face him just yet. His phone started ringing, and that's when I opened one eye to peep at him. He looked at the caller and put his phone back in his pocket. "I know you're awake." he said. I quickly closed my eye back, but it was too late. He came to my side of the bed and slapped my ass hard as hell.

"Ouch, Kevin! What in the world is your problem?" I yelled sitting up in bed. Looking at him, he looked like he was tired as hell. His eyes were low, and they were bloodshot red.

"How the hell did I end up over here?" he said to himself, but I felt the need to answer the question.

"Because you wanted to get all drunk and drive yourself all the way over here last night." I said with an attitude.

"Where the hell is my shirt? You didn't take advantage of me in my sleep did you?" he looked at me with a smirk on his face, and I rolled my eyes. I knew his smirk wasn't going to last forever as soon as I tell him where his shirt was.

"No. I didn't. Your shirt is over there." I said pointing to the corner where his shirt was. The smirk on his face quickly faded as he looked at his balled up shirt.

"What the fuck man? Why you do my shirt like that?" he asked going to pick his shirt up from the floor. I didn't even care that he was mad right now. I laid back down in the bed and turned my back towards him. Hopefully, he would just see himself out, and I could finish getting my beauty sleep. That was wishful thinking, though, because he sat down on the bed beside me.

"We need to talk, Reese." He said with a frustrated sigh. What the hell was he frustrated about? He didn't get cheated on, and I didn't show up at his house last night drunk as hell.

"No we really don't." I mumbled.

"Stop being childish and listen to what the fuck I have to say." he snapped. I looked at him and he had his head down looking sad as hell. I sat up again so he could say what we needed to, then get the hell out.

"Say what you need to say, Kevin." I quietly said.

"I miss you." I rolled my eyes. Now he wants to miss me? He surely didn't miss me when he was fucking his baby mama.

"Okay? You didn't miss me when you were out cheating."

"I know that. I fucked up, and I'm trying to do everything to make sure that never happens again. You're the only woman I want. Shit…" he trailed off looking like he didn't know what he wanted to say. It was cute seeing him all nervous, but I was done with him. I couldn't be with someone who cheated on me. If he did it once, he'd do it again, and I didn't want to go through that.

"You only have one chance to fuck up with me, and you did it. I'm sorry, Kevin, but we can't be together. If I take you back, you'll think it's okay for you to cheat on me again, and I'm not going through that. It was fun while it lasted." The look on his face damn near broke my heart. He looked so sad, it made me almost rethink my answer.

"Aight. I guess you just need some more time." he said standing up and putting his shirt on.

"No, I don't need time. My mind is made up." He didn't say anything. He just looked at me while he put his shoes on.

"No it isn't. You're just talking right now. I'll give you some time to yourself so you can really decide what you want." He came and kissed me on my forehead, then turned to leave. What in the world just happened? I told him I didn't want to be with him anymore, and he forces himself not to believe me. Men, I swear.

As soon as I heard the front door shut, Nikki came prancing into my bedroom. She had a big smile on her face like a young school girl. She came and sat down on my bed and looked at me, but I wasn't in the mood to talk to her right now. I knew she was only in here to talk about Kevin.

"So?" she said waiting for me to tell her something.

"So what?'

"Are y'all two back together?" she cheesed.

"Nope." Her smile instantly faded. She wanted me and him to be together so bad, but I didn't understand why though.

"Why not? What was the point of him coming over here last night?"

"He was drunk, and I was just helping him out." I shrugged my shoulders.

"You know you want that man as much as he wants you."

"Nikki, he cheated on me. Why would I want to be with someone who cheats? Does that even make sense to you?"

"Look how hard he's trying to get you back. That nigga put his life in danger just to come see you. That should mean something to you." I waved her off.

"It should, but it doesn't. None of this would be happening if he would've just kept his dick in his pants in the first place. He knew exactly what he was doing. Now, he's single. I'm done talking about this." I let her know. Kevin was gone, so there was no reason we needed to still be talking about him.

"You guys need to get back together soon. You've turned into a straight bitch since the breakup." I ignored her and got out of bed. I didn't want to be in the house all day, and I especially didn't want to be around Nikki all day either. I needed some more friends other than her. I could hang out with Kaya, but I felt weird knowing that Kevin and I weren't together anymore. I would be asking her so many questions about Kevin, and I know it would get annoying. I needed to find someone who wasn't affiliated with Kevin at all. That shouldn't be too hard, right?

I took a quick shower and threw on a pair of shorts and a plain shirt. I didn't care about looking cute today, because I really didn't have anyone to look cute for anymore. I threw my hair in a low ponytail, then walked out the bathroom. Of course Nikki was still in my room sitting on my bed.

"Where the hell you going? Why didn't you ask if I wanted to go?" she questioned.

"I'm just going for a drive." I looked around my room for my flip-flops and slid them on.

"So. You still could've asked me if I wanted to go with you." I ignored her again and walked out of the room. She was really starting to get on my last nerve, so I had to just leave before I said something to her that I would regret.

Grabbing my keys off the counter, I hurried out the door and did a light jog down the stairs. It was still early in the morning, and it wasn't too hot outside yet. A beautiful day to go for a ride.

"You're in a hurry aren't you?" I heard a voice say. I turned around to see Jay leaning up against the building smoking a cigarette. That's a turn-off. Cigarettes are disgusting, and I didn't understand how or why people smoked them. Gross.

"No, I just needed to get out of my place. I have a friend staying with me right now, and it's starting to get annoying." I said before catching myself. Why do I keep explaining myself to this man like he's my man or something? I really needed to stop doing that. He smiled at me and flicked his cigarette to the ground.

"Where you going?" he asked walking closer to me.

"Just for a drive." Shit. I did it again. I should've told him that I was going to visit family or something. He didn't need to know what I had planned for my day.

"Cool. I'm coming with you."

"Excuse me?" I couldn't have heard him right. There's no way I was letting him come with me. He was an asshole, and I didn't want him anywhere near my car. I didn't want him anywhere near me either.

"You heard me. I ain't got shit to do today, so we can go for a ride. I got gas money if you need it." he told me while pulling out a wad of cash from his pockets. I scoffed. There he goes rubbing his money in my face again like that was supposed to impress me or something.

"No thank you. I can afford my own gas." I snapped walking towards my car.

"I was just trying to be a gentleman." he said following behind me.

"Well, go be a gentleman with some other woman, because you're not coming with me, and your money doesn't impress me at all." He didn't reply to what I said. He just smiled at me while walking to the passenger's side of the car. It was obvious that he was set on coming with me, so I just sucked it up and got in the car.

"Damn, who the hell was sitting up here? There were sitting in the dashboard weren't they?" he laughed while putting the seat all the way back. I stayed quiet as I started the car and drove out of the parking lot.

We had been driving for a good ten minutes with the radio off. I guess it was bothering him because he turned the radio on and started searching through the stations. I kept stealing glances at him, because he was so good looking without even trying. I wonder if he had a girlfriend. I shouldn't have been wondering that, because I would never date him.

"What's up? Why you keep staring at me like that?" he asked. Damn. I was caught.

"Don't flatter yourself. I'm not staring at you." I lied. He chuckled.

"You shouldn't lie. You're not very good at it." I looked over at him, and he was smiling.

"I wasn't lying." I quietly said. He nodded his head and started scrolling through his phone. He was so different from the white boys I'd dated. Cocky as hell too. I mean, he had every reason to be. I bet he was used to females throwing themselves at him all the time. I wasn't going to be one of them though.

"So, Reese's Peanut Buttercup, tell me about yourself." he said without even looking up at me.

"Did you really just call me that?" I laughed.

"Yeah, that's your new name." He looked at me and smiled showing those perfect teeth that he had.

"No it's not. I'm not going to answer to that." I said shaking my head.

"I'll shorten it and call you Peanut. Is that better?"

"What? No! Just call me Reese." He shook his head.

"Nah. I'm calling you Peanut. I like that shit."

"I'm not going to answer to that." He smirked at me.

"You will." he said biting his bottom lip. *Shit.* I thought to myself. *Focus on the road Reese. Focus on the road.* I cleared my throat just as my gas light came on. Of course I needed gas right now. That's not the only thing I was in need of. I need a bathroom because Jay had really opened the floodgates between my legs.

I pulled into the first gas station that I saw. I was going to get me some snacks while I was here, because I didn't eat anything for breakfast. *Maybe I should just go somewhere to get breakfast instead.* Decisions.

"You hungry?" Jay asked. It was like he could read my mind or something.

"Yeah. I was gonna get me some snacks when I went in there." I said taking my seatbelt off. He shook his head and took his seatbelt off too. We got out the car together and walked in the store. Damn. I forgot to see what pump I was on.

"Yeah, let me get twenty on pump three." Jay said handing the cashier the money. I didn't want him to pay for my gas. I was very capable of doing it myself.

"I could've paid for it myself." I whispered to him. He ignored me as he waited for the cashier to give him his change back. She was staring at him a little too hard for my liking. I couldn't say anything because he wasn't my man and would never be my man.

I was shocked when he went around the car to pump my gas. I didn't expect that at all. Such a gentleman and such an asshole at the same time. I smiled.

"You're caught this time. Staring at me all weird and shit." he said. I couldn't even say anything because I was caught, so instead, I just tried to get in the car. He stopped me from doing that, though.

"Get on the other side." he demanded. I looked at him like he was crazy.

"Why?"

"I'm driving. You drive like an old woman." My mouth fell open.

"I do not. I drive like a normal person." I defended.

"Nah, not at all. Get in the car." This time, I listened and went and got in the passenger's seat. I had to adjust the seat since he wanted to put it all the way back. He got in the car and did the same to his seat. He shook his head like he was having a conversation with himself. I was kind of glad he wanted to drive because I really hated driving. I only did it because I had to.

"Where are you taking me?" I asked. "You're not kidnapping me are you?" I smirked.

"Nah. I don't need to kidnap women. They usually just flock to me." He smiled and I rolled my eyes. A ladies' man, just as I expected.

"Right." I chuckled.

"Where you wanna eat at? I'm hungry as hell right now."

"It doesn't matter. As long as I get some food, I'll be happy."

"Fat ass." he muttered to himself.

"I am not a fat ass!" he started laughing like he had told the funniest joke or something.

"I know. You got one though." he winked at me, and once again, the floodgates opened. I quickly looked away from him, because I didn't want him to catch me lusting over him. I was having a hard time controlling myself around him. I quickly looked away from him. Damn it.

He pulled into the drive-thru of Wendy's and I immediately scrunched my face up. I had never eaten there before. My mom used to always say that their food was disgusting, so she wouldn't let me eat it, and I grew up not wanting to eat it.

"What you making that face for?" he asked staring at me with those blue eyes.

"I don't eat here. Never had it, and I never will." I let him know.

"So you don't even know if you like it or not?"

"I know I don't like it." I shrugged.

"Nah, we not about to do this. You're going to try this shit, and I bet you'll like it."

"I bet I won't." I said folding my arms and looking out the window.

"Oh, so you want to make this a bet?" he asked with a raised eyebrow while running his tongue across his bottom lip.

"Sure. I don't really have a lot of money though." He started laughing.

"Nah baby, I don't want your money." he said as I furrowed my eyebrows. "If I win, you have to give me a kiss. If you win, I have to give you one. Deal?" He smiled at me, and I looked at him like he was crazy. I barely knew this man, and he was talking about kissing him. Was I scared? Yes, very.

I was scared, nervous, and excited all at once. I didn't want him to know that though, so I just nodded my head and said,

"Okay." He smiled even harder as he pulled up to give his order.

"Welcome to Wendy's, can I take your order?" the lady said. She sounded like she didn't want to be at work at all. I'll never understand that. Don't be mad at the customers because you don't like your job.

"Yeah, let me get two number ones. I want a Sprite with both orders, and don't put any ice in my shit either." he said. My eyes grew wide in shock. He clearly didn't know how to talk to people.

"Jay!" I yelled. He just looked at me and smirked. The lady told him what the total was, and he pulled up to the window so he could pay.

"What you yelling for?" he asked.

"You obviously don't know how to talk to people." I said shaking my head at him.

"Yes I do. What you talkin' about?"

"Nothing." I waved him off and watched him pay for the food. My stomach was grumbling loudly, and I was praying he didn't hear it. It was highly embarrassing. He handed me the bag and went to go find a place to park.

"You ready to lose this bet?" he inquired with a smile.

"Boy bye, I'm gonna win. I can already tell that I'm not going to like this nasty ass food."

"You don't even know if it's nasty or not." I pulled the burger out of the bag and unwrapped it. I looked at it for a good five minutes, while he was over there tearing his up like he hadn't eaten anything in days.

"You gonna eat or what?" he asked with a mouth full of food. I screwed my face up.

"Don't talk with your mouth full, Jay. That's disgusting." He started laughing.

"Yo, you act more white than I do. That shit crazy." I ignored him and took a small bite of my burger. It was so small, I barely even tasted anything except for the bread. "If you don't stop playing and eat that shit." he demanded. I sighed and took a real bite of the burger. I didn't even want to finish chewing it. I was mad, because it was probably one of the best burgers I had tasted in a long time. It was way better than McDonald's, and that was a fact.

"So?" he asked, staring at me, waiting for a reaction. My face stayed blank.

"It's different." I said.

"Nah, you like that shit! You know you like it, stop playin'!" he was so hype right now, and I was mad because I just lost this bet. I instantly started to feel nervous again. I should've just bet money, not a damn kiss. I didn't feel like I was a good kisser at all.

"I never said I liked it; I said it was different." I said trying to find a way out of this bet. Either way, I was going to have to kiss him. If I lost or if I won. He knew exactly what he was doing when he placed this bet.

We continued to eat in silence, and I had to admit, that was probably the best fast food that I've ever had. I looked over at him, and he was just staring at me with a smirk on his face.

"What, Jay? Why you keep looking at me like that?" I asked annoyed.

"I've never seen someone as beautiful as you." I felt my cheeks get hot, so I looked away from him. I felt silly.

"You say that to all your little girlfriends?" I asked.

"I haven't had a girlfriend since I was in high school. It was always too much drama for me."

"And, how long ago was that?"

"About seven years ago." Seven years? This man has been single for seven years? Damn.

"You don't get lonely?" I know I would.

"Not really. Bitches love me, so I fuck em, then send them on their way. No drama, no crazy phone calls in the middle of the night, and the best part about all of it is I don't have to listen to anyone nagging me. The single life is just so much easier." I shook my head at him.

"That's terrible. I could not be one of the females you mess with." He gave me that infamous smirk again.

"You wouldn't be able to handle me, anyway." he cockily said.

153

"Boy bye. You don't even look like much of a challenge."

"That's what they all say." I chuckled and looked out the window again. "So, about this bet that you lost." He licked his lips, and I felt my whole body get hot.

"What about it?" I was trying to play it cool, but deep down, I was beyond scared.

"Stop playing, girl. I'm waiting." His stare was so intense right now, but I didn't want to look away. I didn't want him to think that I was afraid of him…even though I was. I closed my eyes and leaned in to kiss him. It was a quick peck, but that still counts right?

"What the fuck was that childish ass shit?" he asked once I pulled away. Damn, it didn't count.

"What are you talking about? You said a kiss. You didn't say what kind of kiss it had to be."

"This is how I know you wouldn't be able to handle me. You can't even give me a real kiss." I was getting tired of him saying I couldn't handle him. He didn't know what I could or couldn't handle. I had enough experience with white men, so I knew that I would be able to handle him with ease. I decided to show him, since he liked to run his mouth so much.

In the middle of his laughter, I leaned over and planted my lips on his. He was caught off guard, and at first, he didn't kiss me back. That didn't stop nor discourage me though. I

154

was kissing this man like it was the last time I would ever see him.

He slipped his tongue in my mouth, and I could taste the food he had just finished eating. I felt his hand slide up my shirt and into my bra. He lightly tugged at my nipple causing me to moan against his lips. *Oh shit.* This wasn't going how I expected it to. He was making me want to have sex with him right here, right now. I quickly pulled away and snatched his hand from in my shirt.

"Stop." I said out of breath. I was starting to second guess myself about being able to handle him. I knew he would really mess my head up if we ever had sex. "Why are you staring at me like that?" He was staring at me like he wanted to eat me up.

"Your breath smells like onions, shawty." he said laughing. My hand quickly went to my mouth, covering it. I was beyond embarrassed. I don't even think embarrassed was even the right word to describe how I was feeling right now. I couldn't even say anything back to him.

"Oh my goodness." I said to myself.

"Chill, don't be embarrassed. You were a better kisser than I thought you'd be. I'm glad you stopped me, though, because I was about to bend yo' ass over the hood of this car. I don't give a fuck who was watching either." he said, biting his bottom lip. Is it wrong that I would've let him bend me over the hood of my car? This man was nothing but trouble, and I needed to get away from him before my panties ended up coming off with the rest of my clothes.

Chapter Twelve: Amaya

"That's the girl he's so head over heels for? It looks like she's into that fine ass white boy if you ask me." my best friend Camille said as we sat in the car watching Reese and whoever this white boy was drive off.

"Exactly. The girl isn't even all that." I lied. Reese was beautiful. She was more than beautiful. I don't even think there were any words that I could use to describe how beautiful she was. That's what made me hate her the most. Well, other than she had the man that I wanted. Kevin belonged with me, not her. He couldn't see that for some reason though.

"Girl bye. You know that girl is pretty. They would have some pretty ass babies." I rolled my eyes.

"Kevin and I are going to have pretty ass babies." I couldn't wait to tell Kevin what I saw today at the gas station. It looked like Reese didn't waste any time moving on from Kevin. Maybe once I tell him, he'll realize that I'm the one he needs to be with and not her. He is at my place every night. Not hers. No, we didn't have sex anymore, but that didn't matter. He was still sleeping in my bed beside me.

Last night, he got drunk at my place and decided he wanted to call her. He really called her, professing his love for her and shit like I wasn't standing there. What kind of shit was that? He was in my house! Then, he really left and went to her place. I know because I followed his drunk ass. I know; I was wrong for even letting him get behind the wheel while he was drunk, but he was a grown ass man. He knew what he was doing.

I was heated when I saw Reese come out of her apartment and help Kevin out the car. He spent the night with her and everything. I was so lonely, because I'm used to cuddling with him every night.

"Have you heard from him at all today?" Camille asked.

"No, not really. He still isn't answering his phone, and he's not replying to my text messages. I don't know what his problem is today."

"Do you think he had sex with Reese last night?" That's something I didn't want to think about at all. I'm the only girl he should be having sex with. I'm carrying his child, not Reese.

"I hope not. She's out here being a hoe. That's just nasty." Camille looked at me and laughed.

"Bitch, I know you ain't talking. You were with Greg but you were fucking Kevin. Then, you trapped Kevin by poking holes in his condoms. Now who's the hoe?" she asked. I smacked my lips.

"Shut up. It's not about me right now. It's about getting Kevin to realize that Reese is a hoe. You got the pictures, right?"

"You know I did. My photography skills are on point." She handed me her phone so I could see the pictures that she took of Reese and her new friend. This was going to be great. I couldn't wait to get Kevin over to my place so I could show him these. He probably isn't going to want anything to do with her after this. Then, I would finally have him all to myself.

"I'm hungry. Let's go eat." I said after I sent all of the pictures to my phone.

"Your pregnant ass is always hungry. I'm glad I'm not pregnant. I can't imagine losing my perfect body." I waved her off. Camille did have a perfect body. She was about 5'6 with a stripper booty and the boobs to match. I was sometimes jealous of her because my body wasn't as good as hers. It was alright, because after this pregnancy, I was going to be back and better than ever. I was going to stay in a gym until I got back right. I had to make sure I looked good for Kevin. He couldn't be with a girl that didn't have an amazing body.

"You're gonna end up pregnant, and you're not gonna know who the damn daddy is."

"Fuck you. I'm not getting pregnant, ever. I make sure every nigga I have sex with pulls out." She smiled at me. Camille was a hoe, and she didn't care who knew it. It was almost like she was proud about it too. She never used protection, but claimed she didn't want to get pregnant. She was going to end up pregnant soon. I felt it.

"Why aren't you on birth control or something? Don't you think it would be smart to do that? What if one of these niggas don't pull out and you end up pregnant?" She rolled her eyes at me.

"I'm good. If I get pregnant, I'll just get an abortion. Problem solved." I just shook my head at her. She wasn't going to get an abortion. I knew for a fact she wouldn't get an abortion. When I had got pregnant by Greg, I told her that I planned on getting rid of the baby and she tried her hardest to talk me out of it. Even when I was at the abortion clinic, she was still trying to talk me out of doing it. Once I had gotten the procedure done, she told me how she could never kill an innocent child, blah, blah, blah.

I had to get rid of that child. I didn't want to be with Greg. I was only with him for his money that he was extra stingy with. I needed a man who was going to take care of me and tell me to quit my job. Kevin hasn't told me to quit yet, but I knew he would. I just had to give him time.

We pulled up to McDonalds, and I couldn't wait to eat. The drive-thru line was wrapped around the building, but I wasn't going for that at all. I didn't feel like waiting for my food.

"Damn, this line long as hell. You want to go in?" Camille asked.

"Hell yeah, I wanna go in. I'm too damn hungry to be waiting in line for my food. Then, it looks like they're moving extra slow."

"Fuckin' McDonald's." she mumbled pulling into a park.

It was crazy that I was just running my mouth about Kevin, and here he was sitting in McDonald's at a table by himself. He looked so good in his Nike sweat suit. I wanted to fuck him right there on top of the table he was sitting at.

"Isn't that Kevin right there?" Camille asked.

"Yep." I smiled. My smile faded as I watched Kaya walk to the table and sit down in front of him. I couldn't stand her. Ever since she told me she was fucking Greg, then beat my ass and drug me out of their house, I had nothing but hatred in my heart towards her. Stupid bitch.

"Oh hell no. Who is that bitch he's with? You need to go to their table and cause a scene." she said.

"That's his sister, but I will gladly make my way over there." I smiled to myself as I made my way to their table. I wasn't sure if I should tell Kevin about Reese now or just wait until he came over later. Kaya was the first to see me, and she rolled her eyes so hard, I thought they were going to get stuck. She thought she was better than everybody, but she was nothing but a hoe. Getting paid for sex is hoe behavior. I didn't care what anyone said.

"This bitch." Kaya said loud enough for me to hear. I ignored her as my eyes stayed on Kevin, who hadn't looked up once. He was looking a little sad, and I didn't like that. My baby should be happy at all times. I bet it was Reese's fault that he was looking like this.

"Kevin," I smiled at him. "Why haven't you been replying to my phone calls or texts?" He looked up at me then just shrugged like he didn't care at all. I hated when he started acting like this.

"I don't feel like talking to you, Ma." He said picking up a fry and sticking it into his mouth.

"Why not? You left me last night, and I missed you." I heard Kaya chuckle, so I looked at her with the ugliest expression I could muster up. "You got something you need to say?" I snapped.

"Bitch, you need to go on about your business and let us finish enjoying our meal. I won't hesitate to put my hands on you, pregnant or not. I don't think that baby you're carrying is Kevin's anyway, so I really don't." I rolled my eyes, but I didn't say anything back to her. I knew she wasn't lying about putting her hands on me. That's something that I didn't want to go through again. Getting my ass beat was not a fun experience for me.

"I'm good." Kevin said making me draw my attention back to him and not his ratchet ass sister.

"Are you coming over tonight? We have important things that we need to talk about." I said.

"I don't know. I might, I might not. You being in my face right now while I'm trying to eat is making me not even want to be around you later, so maybe you should get the fuck on." Why the hell was he being so rude right now? Kaya burst into a fit of laughter and that didn't do anything but make me furious. It's like she was enjoying Kevin being ill-mannered to me. I couldn't stand her. Right now, I was wishing that I wasn't pregnant because I would hit her square in the mouth. I didn't care if she beat my ass again or not. She needed someone to pop her in her mouth. Maybe then, she would shut the hell up.

"Why are you being so rude?" I asked folding my arms.

"Why are you still here?" he shot back. I didn't have anything else to say to him. I just turned to leave without even looking at Kaya, who I'm pretty sure had a smile on her face.

"What happened? Why you looking so sad?" Camille asked when I walked back over to her. I just looked at her and rolled my eyes. Why didn't she come to the table with me? Maybe, she could've helped me not look so damn stupid. I always knew her ass was scary; I just never wanted to believe it.

"Let's go. I'm not even hungry anymore." I uttered walking out of the building.

"Amaya, what the hell? I'm hungry!" she yelled after me, but I disregarded her and kept walking towards the car. Foolish wasn't even the word to describe how I was feeling right now. I was just ready to go home and smoke. I know, I wasn't supposed to be smoking or drinking while I was pregnant, but I didn't care. I was doing it anyway. Shit, I'm only three months pregnant anyway. It wasn't going to harm the baby.

"You are so damn emotional. I'll be happy when you have this baby." she said starting the car.

"Just shut up!" I snapped. She pursed her lips and looked at me like she wanted to say something, but then decided against it. Good. I didn't want to hear her talking anyway. She was really annoying me right now.

The ride back to my place was a silent one. I guess she was feeling some type of way because I yelled at her, but she would get over it. She was a grown ass woman, and it wasn't even that serious.

"I guess I'll see you later." she said without even looking at me. *Yeah, whatever bitch.* I thought to myself. I got out the car and slammed the door just to piss her off even more than she already was. Yeah, I was petty, and I damn sure didn't care.

"Stupid hoe." I said unlocking my door. As soon as I got into my place, I felt sluggishly tired. I really wanted to roll me a blunt and smoke it, but my bed was calling me right now. Stripping down to nothing but my underwear, I got in bed and was out like a light before my head could hit the pillow.

I was in a deep sleep until loud banging coming from my front door woke me up.

"Ugh, who the fuck is here?" I asked getting out of bed and making my way to the door. Looking out of the peephole, I saw Kevin standing there looking good as always. I smiled and quickly opened the door to let my soon to be man in.

"Damn, what the fuck took you so long to open the door? And, why the hell you opening the door all naked and shit?" he asked walking past me so he could go sit down on the couch.

"Nigga, I was sleep. I can answer the door however I want." I said with a smirk.

"Get ya ass beat if you want to." I ignored him as I went into the kitchen to get me some wine. I wanted some Patron, but I didn't have any right now. I needed to take my ass to the liquor store to get some.

"I'm shocked you even came. You were being a real asshole earlier." I said sitting down beside him. He looked at me, then looked at the wine glass that I had in my hand.

"The fuck you doing?" he asked.

"I'm drinking. What does it look like, nigga?" I said with an eye roll. He clearly saw what I was doing. There was no point to even ask.

"You're pregnant! The fuck you drinking for?"

"Why do you even care? You don't even want this baby to be yours anyway." I said taking a sip of my drink while staring at him. Before I could even react, he slapped the glass out of my hand causing the wine to spill all over me and the glass to shatter, as it hit the floor.

"What the fuck, Kevin?!" I shrieked.

"Why the hell you drinking knowing you got a damn baby inside of you? There's a possibility that this baby could be mine, and if it comes out all fucked up because of you, I'm beating your ass!" he boomed, standing over me.

"You're so damn extra!" was all I said as I got up so I could clean this wine off of me. He followed me to my bedroom.

"Don't even want you to carry my damn child." he tried to whisper, but I heard him anyway.

"Oh? Who do you want to carry your child? Little miss perfect, Reese? Nah. She's going to be having mixed babies with a white man." I smiled while our eyes locked.

"Fuck you talkin' bout?" he asked with a confused look on his face.

"Your girlfriend is with a white boy." I could tell by the look on his face that he didn't believe a damn word that I was saying, so I grabbed my phone and went to the pictures that I had of Reese. "Here." I said shoving the phone in his face. He snatched the phone from out my hand and stared hard at the picture. I watched as his face turned a crimson color. Mission accomplished.

"Hell nah. When the fuck was this?" he quietly asked.

"Earlier today. I saw her when I was out with Camille, and I had to take a picture. You're over here stressing about a hoe who doesn't even give a fuck about you. It's obvious that you're not her type. You're not white enough for her, Kevin." I said with a laugh. Kevin gritted his teeth and threw my phone against the wall, causing it to shatter.

"Shut the fuck up, Amaya! This is why we could never be together. You're fucking crazy! You were probably following her around because that's some crazy ass shit you would do!" he yelled causing me to jump at his sudden outburst.

"You broke my damn phone!" I yelled back. He was so disrespectful today. He hasn't even been here for a full thirty minutes, and my phone was the second thing he's shattered.

"Fuck that phone, bruh." he walked out of my room and I followed right behind him.

"Where are you going?" I asked once I saw him heading toward the door.

"I'm out, yo. I can't deal with bitches right now." He left out the door and slammed it behind him causing one of my pictures to fall. What was he mad at me for? Reese was the one that was caught with another man. All I did was get the pictures of it, and he wanted to be mad at me? I just didn't understand men. They were complicated as hell. He would be back, though. He always came back, and I was going to be right here waiting on him too.

Chapter Thirteen: Kevin

Mad was a fucking understatement right now. I was already in a bad mood because Reese wasn't fucking with me, but it got even worse once Amaya showed me that picture of Reese and that white boy. I didn't know what it was with her and white boys, but I planned on finding out who this nigga was and beating his ass. Reese had me so fucked up right now. I know I fucked up, but she wasn't supposed to move on that fast. She was supposed to stay her ass single and realize that I'm the nigga for her. Not these bitch ass white men.

I broke all types of traffic laws as I sped to Reese's apartment complex. She was going to talk to me and let me know everything I needed to know about this fuck ass white boy. I needed to know where the fuck he lived, so I could personally show up to his crib and beat his ass. Stupid ass nigga was fucking with the wrong one.

Pulling up to the apartments, I parked illegally and jumped out the car. I really wished I was high right now, because that would probably calm me down and keep me from doing some crazy shit, but it was too late for that now. I was already here, and I didn't have any weed on me, either. Fuck it.

Jogging up the stairs, I stopped in front of Reese's door and debated if I was going to knock or just try to kick this bitch down. I didn't want to cause a scene and have her nosey ass neighbors out here all in our business and shit, but I knew it was going to happen anyway.

"Reese!" I yelled, banging on the door. "Open this fuckin' door, yo!" I heard movement coming from inside, and I kept banging until the door swung open. There stood an angry Reese, but she didn't have anything to be mad about. I was the one that needed to be mad.

"What in the world is wrong with you? Why are you banging on my door like you're crazy?" she snapped. She was looking so good, it was breathtaking. Almost making me forget what I came here to do. I stepped into the apartment and closed the door behind me.

"You moved on that fast, huh? You couldn't wait for me to fuck up so you could go out and be a hoe!" I yelled getting in her face.

"Excuse me?!" her little voice shouted back. "You're the one that cheated, but I'm the hoe? How? I'm single! I can do whatever the hell I want!"

"Who the fuck is he? Where the fuck does that bitch nigga live at?" She looked at me confused like she was trying to figure out who the hell I was talking about. Damn, she had that many dudes lined up?

"Who are you talking about, Kevin?" I ignored her and walked into her bedroom.

"That nigga in here?! Where the fuck he at?" I opened her closet door and start pulling shit out. Her closet was small, but maybe he was hiding in here. I hoped he was.

"Kevin! What are you doing?!" she shrieked, as she watched me throw all her clothes and shoes out of the closet, and onto her bedroom floor. I continued to ignore her as I snatched all of the covers off the bed. I was checking to see if there were any stains, because I know for a fact Reese messes up the bed every time we had sex. The shit was clean though. I walked out of the bedroom and went straight for the kitchen.

I opened the cabinets and start pulling the pots and pans out. Maybe this nigga could fit in the cabinets. Shit, I was on a rampage, and there was no stopping me right now.

"Kevin!" she yelled, but her screams were falling on deaf ears right now. I pulled the glasses out of the top cabinets and threw them on the floor, causing each and every one of them to break. "Stop it! Stop it! Stop it!" she cried.

"Where that nigga at, Reese?" I yelled again.

"Who? Who the hell are you talking about? There's nobody here but us!" She had tears streaming down her face, but I ignored them as I walked into her living room and flipped one of the couches over, causing it to fall onto the glass table she had in the middle of the floor. It shattered into pieces, and Reese let out a gut wrenching scream.

"Where the fuck that white boy that you was with earlier at, Reese? Huh? Where the fuck is his white ass?!"

171

Reese was crying hard as hell. Something that I had never seen before.

"You talkin' bout me, homie?" a voice said from behind me. I turned around seeing the same white boy from the pictures Amaya showed me. He stood at the door like he was ready for war. Shit, I was ready too.

Without any talking, I charged at his ass and caught him right in the mouth. I expected him to back down after I swung, but to my surprise, he didn't. He came back swinging getting me in my jaw. After that, we went blow for blow in Reese's living room, fucking it up even more. I could hear Reese crying and screaming for us to stop, but right now, I wanted to kill this nigga with my bare hands. He was doing a pretty good job with keeping up with me, even when I was on top.

"Kevin! Get off that white boy before I shoot you in the ass!" I heard Kaya yell. That made me stop what I was doing to look at her. When the hell did she get here and how did she know where I was even at? I looked over at Reese, who had my phone in her hand and realized she was the one who called Kaya. "You always doing some shit, Kevin. Look what you did to this girl's apartment!" Kaya yelled at me. She helped me up off the floor, and I watched Reese go over to the white boy and help him off the floor. That only enraged me even more.

"Man…" I trailed off looking around Reese's place. I really fucked it up. All I wanted to do was find out who this white boy was, and I took shit too far. Way too far.

"You'll be lucky if she ever talks to you again. Let's go." Kaya snapped. I looked at Reese one last time who was looking at me with tears in her eyes.

"Reese, I'm sorry, man." I quietly said while looking at the floor.

"Get out! Get the hell out, Kevin!" I didn't say anything else. I just slowly followed Kaya out of the apartment. She didn't say anything to me until we were inside my car.

"What the hell were you thinking, Kevin? Why did you destroy her place like that? You need anger management, my nigga." she said.

"How the hell you get over here?" I wondered.

"I was over at that store with Clay when she called me from your phone. I couldn't understand what she was saying because she was crying so bad, but I heard her say your name and that I needed to come get you. I didn't expect to walk in on you beating the white boy's ass." she said shaking her head.

"I fucked up man." I blew out a frustrated breath thinking about how Reese will probably never want to talk to me again after this.

"Yeah. You really did. Be glad she called me and not the police. If your black ass would've went to jail, you would've stayed in there for a couple of days. You need to really learn how to control your anger." She was the one to talk.

"Says the one who slit a girl's throat."

"Fuck you." she spat. I laughed because she knew she was just as crazy as I was. She just was a little better than me at controlling it.

"What do you think I should do? I know she's not going to want to talk to me ever again, but I need that girl, Kaya." Kaya looked at me and smiled.

"Someone has been bitten by the love bug."

"Shut the fuck up with that gay shit, man."

"How is that gay? You fell for that girl hard as hell. I never thought I'd see the day." She pinched my cheek, and I slapped her hand away.

"Chill. I'm being serious right now." I said stopping at a red light.

"I don't know, Kevin. I guess I could call her tomorrow and try talking to her, but I'm not making any promises. I don't know if she's going to want to talk to you or not." she shrugged.

"Something is better than nothing." I responded looking out the window.

"What's good, nigga?" I heard Royal yell. He was in the car next to us with a light-skinned bitch in the front seat.

"What's up, fool? Where you headed?"

"Shit, I'm going on a date. I'm feeling real classy tonight." he said smiling. The girl in the front seat wasn't even cute. I knew he was just trying to fuck anyway. The light turned green, and we said our goodbyes and drove off.

"That nigga crazy." I said laughing. Kaya didn't say anything. She just looked down at her hands looking sad as hell. "Oh damn, Kay. I forgot how you felt about that nigga."

"It's okay." she said quietly without even looking up. She was sad as hell and I wasn't used to it.

"Have y'all talked at all?"

"Nope. He doesn't answer when I call or text him. He's clearly moved on and out are enjoying life." She wiped a tear that fell, and I didn't know how to feel. Royal was my nigga and all, but I didn't fuck around when it came to Kaya. I didn't want to cause any problems, because that was their relationship, but I've never seen her cry until now so this was a problem for me.

"I'll talk to that nigga for you." I let her know. She looked at me with wide eyes.

"No! Don't do that! I'm not desperate, and that's what you're going to make it seem like."

"Man, fuck all that shit. You over here crying and shit, so I know it's serious. I'm talking to that nigga tomorrow. I don't care how you feel about it either." She didn't say anything else. She just folded her arms and pouted like a big ass baby. "Stop pouting. I'm not even going to make it seem like you want me to talk to him. I got this." She rolled her eyes and looked out the window.

"Whatever." she mumbled.

The next day, I woke up around noon. It was probably because I didn't get much sleep last night because I was up worrying about Reese. I still didn't know who that white boy was to her, and I needed to find out ASAP. I was glad I beat his ass, even though he got me one good time in my lip. I called her over twenty times. She eventually got tired of sending me to voicemail and just turned her phone off altogether. I needed Kaya to go over there and talk to her right now. I just wanted Reese back.

I sighed heavily before sitting up in bed. I know Amaya was waiting for me to come back, but I was too pissed to go back last night. It was her fault that I went to Reese's house acting a fool. I was starting to wish she would've never shown me those pictures, but at the same time, I was glad that she did. Shit was crazy as fuck.

Once I was showered and dressed, I decided to go see what was going on with Rome at his shop since I hadn't been in a couple of days. Kaya was downstairs watching TV, and that shocked me.

"What you doing here?" I asked. She looked up at me with sad eyes, but tried to cover it up with a smile.

"I came around four this morning. I couldn't sleep, and I didn't want to be alone." I sighed.

"How many times you called Royal last night?" She looked down.

"A lot." I heard her sniffle and the shit pissed me off.

"Man, I'll be back." I said, grabbing my car keys and heading out the door. I needed to have a talk with Royal. He was the one who fucked up, but he was acting like Kaya did it. They both just needed to sit down and talk it out. They needed to decide if they were going to be together or not, because I was tired of seeing Kaya sad over this nigga.

Walking into the tattoo shop, Brandi looked at me and rolled her eyes. I wasn't about to entertain her ass today, though. I wasn't trying to deal with any females unless it was Reese, and she probably wasn't trying to deal with me. Shit was all fucked up right now.

"What's good, nigga?" Rome said as I walked into the back. Royal was sitting on the couch drinking a beer. I ignored Rome and walked right over to Royal.

"Nigga, let me holla at you right quick." I said standing over Royal. His mood instantly changed when he saw I wasn't smiling or in a good mood.

"What's up?" he said putting his beer down and standing up, ready for whatever.

"What's going on with you and my sister?" he chuckled and waved me off.

"Not a damn thing."

"So what? You done with her? You could be a man and let her know what's up instead of having her crying over yo' ass." Again, he chuckled.

"Why worry about one bitch, when I can have multiple bitches?" I looked at this nigga like he was crazy before I just snapped and punched him dead in his shit.

"Yo! Chill the fuck out!" Rome yelled as Royal and I fought. Damn. I was fighting again. I was only supposed to be talking to this nigga. Not fighting his bitch ass. Rome pushed me to one side of the room, then he pushed Royal to the other side. "What the fuck?!" Rome yelled.

"All this over a bitch?" Royal asked.

"Stop calling my sister a bitch, nigga! Fuck is your problem?" I felt myself getting mad all over again.

"Chill out, both of y'all! Royal, get the fuck out your feelings. You were just basically crying over here a couple of weeks ago. Now that she actually wants yo crybaby ass again, you wanna flex on her?" Rome yelled. Royal didn't say anything. He just looked down. He knew damn well he still wanted Kaya. He was being childish as hell right now. "And you," Rome said turning toward me. "Stay out they business!"

"Man, fuck that! That's my fuckin' sister! I've never seen her cry before until she got with this bitch ass nigga!" Royal looked like he wanted to say something, but he decided against it.

"Y'all need to squash this shit right now." I looked at Rome like he was crazy.

"Nah." I said shaking my head and walked out of the building. I was acting out of character right now. I knew it was all because Reese wasn't fucking with me. I needed to get my girl back, man.

Chapter Fourteen: Kaya

"Fuck these niggas. They ain't shit but some good dick, sometimes." I said to myself as I walked around Kevin's kitchen looking for something to eat. This nigga didn't have shit to eat in here, and I was starving. I guess I was going to have to go out and get something to eat. As I grabbed my car keys, Reese popped in my head, so I decided to give her a call.

"Hello?" she quietly said into the phone.

"Hey, it's Kaya." I said as I got into my car.

"Oh, hi."

"I'm just calling to see how you were doing after last night. Do you need anything? I can stop by if you'd like." She cleared her throat.

"Yeah, you can do that. I need someone to talk to." I nodded my head as if she could see me.

"Okay. I'll be over there in about fifteen minutes." I ended the call and drove off heading in the direction of her place. I still couldn't believe Kevin went to her house acting a damn fool last night. Well... actually, I could believe it. That nigga has a few screws missing. My phone started ringing, and it was Kevin.

"Yes, Kevin?"

"Mannn, I fucked up." he sighed. I rolled my eyes.

"What the hell you do now?"

"I fought Royal." I almost swerved into the other lane after what he had told me.

"What?! Why? What the fuck, Kevin?"

"That nigga pissed me off. I feel bad about it now. That's my nigga. I shouldn't be fighting him." I shook my head.

"What's going on with you? You're really grumpy like you're on your period or some shit."

"Reese, bruh." he sounded so sad.

"I'm on my way to her place right now to talk shit about you." he sighed again.

"I'm gonna talk to you later." He hung up before I could even say anything back. He was in his feelings about Reese while I was in my feelings about Royal. This nigga tried so hard to get me to talk to him, and now when I'm ready, he's ignoring me. What the fuck?

He was making me feel like a little bitch. I'd never done no shit like this. I never had to call a nigga more than twice, because they always answered the first time. Niggas chased me, I didn't have to chase them. It was a different story with Royal though. I didn't understand him, but I feel like Kevin made shit worse by fighting him.

I pushed the thoughts of Royal to the back of my mind as I pulled into Reese's apartment complex. I needed to get myself together and go back to my old ways. These niggas ain't shit. I was better off just taking their money and going on about my day. I fucked up when I met Royal.

"Hi." Reese softly said, as she opened her door for me. Her eyes were red and puffy like she had just finished crying. I stepped into her apartment and instantly felt bad. Her place was still in shambles, and it was all Kevin's fault.

"How are you feeling? Want me to stay and help you clean up?" I really didn't want to help her, since I wasn't the one who caused this, but I was just being nice.

"No, it's okay. I meant to start on it last night, but I couldn't. That was way too much for me." I nodded my head and went to go sit on the couch that wasn't flipped over.

"He has real anger issues. I'm not trying to make excuses for him or anything, though."

"He came in here asking about another man. I'm not with anyone. I still haven't gotten over him yet; why would I be with someone else? That's why he came in here and fucked everything up. He was looking for a man. He broke all of my dishes, Kaya. I don't have a lot of money like y'all do. It's going to be expensive as hell to get everything back that he destroyed." Her eyes start watering up, and I didn't know what to do or say. I hated when people cried in front of me. It made me feel awkward and weird.

"I can give you the money to pay for everything if you need me to." I offered. She quickly shook her head no.

"No. It's not your fault that he came in here acting a fool. I'll get everything myself." There was a knock at the door, and she got up to answer it. The same white boy from last night walked in holding a bag of Chinese food.

"Oh, I didn't know you were gonna have company. I would've gotten more food." he said looking at me.

"It's alright. I already ate." I lied, knowing damn well I was over here about to die from hunger. His face was messed up. You could tell he had been in a fight, but he was still fine as hell. There was no denying that. White men weren't my type though.

"I didn't know you were going to come over today." Reese said taking the bag out of his hand.

"I came to see how you were doing. You seemed really sad last night when I left." She smiled at him.

"I was, but I'm okay now." He smiled back at her. I could tell he had some type of feelings for her. I didn't know if the feeling was mutual with her, but she looked at him like she wanted to have sex with him right here, right now, not even caring that I was in the room.

"Cool. You need help cleaning this up? I can hire somebody to do it for you." he said.

"No, it's okay. I can do it myself." she said going to put the food down on the counter.

"I know I asked, but now I'm telling you. I'm hiring somebody to clean this shit up for you. You don't have to pay for shit; I gotchu." he said winking at her. *Damn.* I thought to myself. It was sexy as hell how he just bossed up on her like that. She couldn't do anything but smile at him.

I was starting to wonder who this white boy was. Is she planning on fucking with him next? Is this why Kevin beat his ass last night? I had to admit, if they did get together, they would make a cute ass couple.

"I'm Jay." he said, walking over to me with his hand out so I could shake it.

"Kaya. I don't shake people's hands. That's nasty." I said, looking at his hand in disgust. He chuckled and put his hand down to his side. I didn't care if he felt some type of way. People don't be washing their hands sometimes, so I didn't shake hands. Better safe than sorry.

"I feel it." he said. "I was just stopping by to check on you. I'll be back a little later." he told Reese, then made his way out the apartment. Reese was smiling like a school girl. She was feeling that white boy. Kevin wasn't going to be happy at all once I told him this.

"So... Who was that?" I asked.

"He's just a neighbor. A really nice neighbor."

"You sure about that? You were staring at him kinda hard." I pulled out my mirror to check my face. I didn't have on any makeup, so I was feeling really naked right now. I usually never left the house with a bare face. That just wasn't my thing.

"Yes, I'm sure. I'm not looking at another man like that until I'm fully over Kevin. Who knows how long that's going to take?" she said with a roll of her eyes.

"Will you ever talk to him again?" I don't know why I told Kevin that I would do this. I felt like I was all in their business. He's the one that needs to be over here fixing this, not me.

"Probably not," she said looking at the mess he made. "I have nothing to say to his crazy ass. He's just too much for me."

"I think you should at least hear him out." I suggested. She shrugged her shoulders.

"I don't know. He showed me that he's crazy as hell. Why would I want to be with someone who's like that? What if he gets so mad to the point he ends up putting his hands on me?"

"If he does that, I'll personally beat his ass myself." She started laughing, but I was serious. Reese was a sweet girl. She didn't know what she was getting herself into when she started fucking with Kevin.

"I just need time to focus on myself. I'm not worried about a relationship right now." I fought the urge to roll my eyes at her. That's what every female says after they go through a bad breakup. I didn't understand it, though. Why weren't you already focused on yourself? You can be in a relationship and still focus on yourself. Shit, I damn sure did it while I was with Royal.

I stayed at Reese's house for another thirty minutes before I decided to leave. She was acting all sad, and it was starting to make me feel sad about my situation with Royal. Fuck him, though. I had to say that to myself at least twenty times a day. As soon as I got in my car, my phone begin to ring.

"Hello?" I said, answering the phone without looking at who was calling.

"Kaya." Royal sighed into the phone. My heart dropped to the pit of my stomach as I quickly hung up. *Oh, now you want to talk to me after you and my brother fought? Hell no. It doesn't work that way.* I was done playing these games with him. I was going to push him to the back of my head, and he was going to stay there. Picking my phone back up, I dialed Clay's number and waited for her to answer.

"Yes Kay-Kay?" she answered.

"Bitch, what I tell you about calling me that stupid ass nickname?" I hated when she called me that.

"I know; I just love getting on your nerves."

"Let's go out tonight. I need to drink and turn the fuck up." I said getting excited about being drunk.

"Where you wanna go? It's not going to be that fun, because my pregnant ass can't drink." Damn. I forgot she wouldn't be able to drink.

"Umm, I'll invite Reese to come with us." I let her know.

"Who the hell is Reese?"

"Kevin's ex-girlfriend. She's sad over their breakup and shit, and I'm trying to get over a fuck nigga. The turn up needs to be real tonight. I wanna get so drunk that I don't even remember tonight."

"Okay. I'm driving since you wanna drink and shit." she said, and I chuckled.

"Duh, bitch." We talked for a couple more minutes before I ended the call. I had a couple of text messages from Royal, but I deleted them without even reading what they said. He wasn't worth it anymore. He wanted to be childish, then he could do that by himself.

Pulling off, I dialed Reese's number so I could ask her if she wanted to go out tonight.

"Hello? Is everything okay?" she asked.

"Yeah girl, what you got planned for tonight?"

"Um, I was just going to have a movie night with one of my friends…" she trailed off.

"One of your friends? It wouldn't happen to be that fine ass white boy, would it?" I had to ask. I could see it in her eyes that she wanted to get down and dirty with that man. I knew it was none of my business, but I wanted to know anyway.

"No," she laughed. "It's my best friend, Nikki."

"Oh, well I'm planning on going out to the club tonight. I want you and your friend to come with me."

"Really? Okay, I gotta find me something to wear." She ended the call, and I could tell she was excited as hell to go out tonight. She probably didn't get out much, so this was going to be good for her. Shit, it was going to be good for me, too. I couldn't wait to get drunk. I needed to go find me something to wear too. It was a must that I had to be the best looking woman in the club tonight, but first, I needed to go get me something to eat.

***

"Damn, bitch. You had all day to find you an outfit. Why are you just now starting to look for one?" Clay asked me as I stood in my closet looking for a cute outfit.

"Because, I needed your help, and you wanted to take all damn night to get here." I said, pulling out my favorite nude dress.

"Rome wasn't trying to let me leave. He wanted to have sex like five times, then I ended up falling asleep. Shit, it's hard being pregnant." I looked at her and rolled my eyes,

"Bitch, you ain't even showing yet." Clay was still skinny as hell. If you didn't know her, you wouldn't even know that she was pregnant.

"So! I still be tired. Now, hurry up and find something to wear. I'm not trying to stand in line all night. Not in these shoes." I waved her off and slipped my dress on. Royal hated when I wore this dress. It was short as hell, damn near a shirt, and it struggled to hold my boobs in. I loved the way I looked in it though. Sexy as hell.

"I'm wearing this." I smiled to myself as I looked in the mirror.

"You can tell you're single. No nigga would let you walk out the house with that on." Clay said scrolling through her phone. I stuck my tongue out at her and went to the closet to find some shoes to wear.

"Fuck these niggas." I said putting on a pair of black heels. I was looking good, and I knew it. My makeup looked like it was professionally done, my long, black weave was curled to perfection, and my body looked like I paid for it. I'm taking somebody's nigga tonight. No fucks were about to be given.

"Kevin's calling you." Clay said, holding my phone in her hand. She handed me the phone.

"What now nigga? You calling to tell me you did some more crazy shit?" I asked.

"No, nigga. I'm calling to see what you're doing tonight." I could hear a female's voice in the background, and it sounded like that crazy bitch Amaya. I couldn't stand her at all. I was hoping like hell that the baby she was carrying didn't belong to Kevin. He didn't need those type of problems.

"I'm going to the club tonight with Clay."

"Oh word? Shit, I ain't got shit to do, tonight. I might show up too. I'll hit you up later." He ended the call before I could even say anything back.

"Kaya! Why'd you let him know where we're going? Rome doesn't know that I planned on going to the club with you tonight. He thinks we're just chillin' at your place." Clay frantically said.

"Really, bitch? Why didn't you just tell him that we're going out? You know he's gonna be calling you every hour anyway, so how was that about to work?" She obviously didn't think this whole thing through. She should've just told him what we had planned.

"You know damn well he wasn't gonna let my pregnant ass go to the club. Especially without him. I didn't want him to come to the club with us. He's gonna fuck up my fun." she pouted. Oh well. I'm pretty sure that nigga is going to be there since Kevin was.

"Maybe he won't show up." I tried to reason, but we both knew that he was going to be there.

"And maybe Royal won't show up." she said, sarcastically.

"He and Kevin fought earlier, so he might not. Even if he does, I really don't give a fuck. Fuck his childish ass. I'm going to turn up, not worry about a fuck boy who doesn't know what he wants in life."

"What you mean they fought? Like an argument fight, or these niggas were really shooting them shits?"

"They fought bitch. Wasn't no arguing. Kevin called and told me right after it happened. I hope Kevin beat his ass too." I said with a hair flip.

"Girl, stop. You sounding bitter as hell right now." she said laughing. She got up to look at herself in the mirror. She had on a black jumpsuit that was tight as hell. I already knew that Rome was going to have a problem with her outfit when he saw her. She wasn't going to be able to have any fun tonight.

"Damn, I look good." she said to herself. She was looking good. We both were. I was determined to have a good night tonight. Reese had already texted me and told me she was there, so Clay and I were on our way.

Of course, the line was wrapped around the building, but I never had to stand in line. The bouncers loved me for some reason, so they would always let me in with no questions asked.

"It looks like it's packed in here. I don't got time to be standing too close to people, especially if they stink." Clay complained.

"Girl, shut up, and come on." We got out the car and made our way to the entrance. Everyone was staring at Clay and me as we walked. I was used to getting stared at, especially when I was at work, so this was nothing to me. I knew half the bitches in line were probably talking shit about us, but I didn't care. They could talk all they wanted. They weren't putting any money in my damn pockets.

The bouncer looked at us, and immediately let us in, like I knew they would. I was looking way too good to be standing in line, and he probably felt the same way.

"Who are they? Why don't they have to stand in line?" I heard someone yell. I just flipped my hair and kept it moving. If I had to stand in line, I'd be mad too.

"These bitches mad." Clay said as I laughed. Bitches will always be mad. It's like they don't have anything better to do with their lives. That wasn't my problem, though.

Clay and I headed straight towards the bar, even though she couldn't drink. I was going to get sloppy drunk, and I didn't even care. I ordered three shots of Patron, while Clay got some water, and I felt bad for her. I didn't plan on getting pregnant ever again. I needed to be able to drink, and nine months without liquor wasn't going to work for me.

"It's obvious you don't have a man, because you wouldn't be over here buying drinks for yourself." I heard a voice say. I turned to see a light-skinned nigga standing beside me with dreads and tattoos on his face. He was alright looking, but I liked my men dark. He could buy me drinks if he wanted, but that's all I was going to let him do.

"I don't." I smiled at him ready to flirt. Clay grabbed my wrist causing me to turn and look at her.

"I know that nigga from somewhere." she said into my ear.

"Really? He's kinda cute, but you know I don't fuck with these light bright ass niggas." I laughed taking a shot.

"He just looks really familiar, and I don't know where I know him from." I shrugged my shoulders and turned my attention back to Mr. Light Bright.

"Can I buy you a drink?" he asked just like I knew he would.

"Nigga, you can buy me the whole bar." He laughed, but I was so serious. I loved how he was spending his money on me. I'd rather spend other people's money anyway.

"Come on, Kaya. I think you've had enough." Clay said getting off the bar stool and trying to help me off mine. It had been about fifteen minutes since we got here, and I've had more shots than I could even count. As long as ole boy was buying them, I was drinking them.

"I'm goooood." I slurred barely being able to stand up.

"Damn, you're leaving already?" he asked.

"No, come with meee." He didn't have a problem with that at all. He followed right behind me as Clay drug me into the crowd.

"Where are you taking me?" I giggled.

"Kevin texted you and said he was in VIP. You need to sit down and chill for a minute." Clay said. Sit down? I'd been sitting down since we got here. I was ready to turn up.

"Kaya!" I saw Reese coming up to me. She had on a short, black, strapless dress looking good as hell. I could tell she wasn't comfortable in what she was wearing though. She kept tugging at her dress trying to pull it down.

"Come on!" I said pulling her to VIP with us. I felt like I was floating right now. I wanted to smoke though. Hopefully, Kevin had some weed. He always did.

We finally made it to VIP, and I couldn't have been happier. There were way too many people walking around and bumping into me. I was starting to get pissed off.

"Kevin!" I yelled excited to see him. I was shocked to see Amaya sitting on his lap. Why was that stupid bitch even here? She wasn't invited. I purposely pushed her off his lap and gave him a big hug like I hadn't seen him in years.

"What the fuck?!" Amaya yelled, but I just ignored her stupid ass.

"Kaya, how much have you had to drink?" he asked.

"Not enough!" he looked at me and shook his head. I saw Rome walk over to Clay and pull her off to the side. The look he had on his face wasn't a pleasant one at all. I knew he was more upset about her outfit than her actually being here.

I spotted a bottle of Patron on the table and picked it up. I was about to drink from this bottle and not give a fuck. I was happy right now, and I had more liquor. Yes, it was definitely a good night.

"You didn't tell me Kevin was going to be here." Reese whispered in my ear. It had totally slipped my mind that they were going to be around each other tonight. Before I could even say anything, Kevin was up making his way over to Reese. I just shrugged my shoulders. She was gonna have to face him eventually.

I turned to talk back to the couches and spotted the last person I wanted to see. Royal. He was sitting there, looking good as hell of course, with a bitch on his lap. He was rubbing up and down her thighs as she giggled. I looked at the girl and got mad as hell. There sat Cherry smiling like a fucking Cheshire Cat. Stupid bitch. Royal and I locked eyes, and I looked away from him. I continued to act unbothered even though I was clearly bothered. Why was he even here? When did he and Kevin become cool again? Why did he have that stupid bitch sitting on his lap? It was obvious he had a thing for strippers, because she works at the same place I work.

"You might need to slow down with the drinks." Light Bright said. I forgot that I had even told him to come with me to VIP. I just smiled at him.

"Nope. I'm good." The song changed, and everyone in the club got hype as hell. Even I got hype as hell. I started grinding on Light Bright with the bottle of Patron in my hand. I still didn't even know what his name was, but I honestly didn't care to find out. He would be forgotten by the time morning got here. He grabbed my hips, pressing himself into me. This was just too much fun right now. Well, I was having fun until I got snatched away from him. I expected it to be Royal who pulled me away from him, but it wasn't. It was Kevin. He was looking mad as hell right now.

"Kevin, what the hell?" I yelled. He ignored me as Rome walked up, gun drawn and everything.

"Nigga, you following me or some shit?" Rome asked, pointing his gun directly at Light Bright. What the hell was going on? Out the corner of my eye, I saw Royal getting up and coming over to where Rome was.

"I heard you've been looking for me, nigga." Royal smiled. Damn, he looked good in all that Gucci he had on. Clay pulled me away from all the shit that was going on.

"That's Rome's brother! That's how I know him!" she yelled. Reese came over to us with her friend I guess she invited.

"Y'all, this is my friend Nikki." She smiled. Clay's whole body tensed up, and I didn't understand why until I looked at her friend. Nikki. Oh, I'd been waiting to catch this bitch. I could tell by the look on her face that she was shocked to see us. That shock didn't last very long, because I took the Patron bottle that was in my hand and hit her with it. The bottle shattered and liquor went everywhere as she fell to the ground.

"Kaya!" I heard Reese yell. From that point on, I didn't hear a thing that anyone said to me. I was beating Nikki's ass and had blacked out. The last thing I remember is Kevin pulling me off of her and me being drug out of the club.

"Chill out!" he yelled at me. I was trying my hardest to get away from his grasp. I wanted to go back in there and finish what I started. She had been fucking with my friend for too long, and since Clay couldn't get to her, I was going to do it for her.

"Let me go, Kevin!" I yelled. I saw Light Bright being drug out the club too, but he was badly beaten and looked like he was barely breathing. What the hell happened to him? My question was soon answered when I saw Royal come out the club yelling and shit. He was hype as hell, and his shirt was off.

"Let's go, Kaya! Pull your fucking dress down!" I looked down at myself realizing my dress had risen showing my black thong that I was wearing. It didn't really bother me that much, but I knew it made Kevin uncomfortable. He finally let me go, and I pulled my dress down, still drunk as hell. "Get yo' ass in the car." he demanded. I didn't even say anything to him. I just did as he said, ready to go because I felt like I was about to pee on myself.

He walked back over to where Royal was and tried to calm him down. It didn't make sense to me. How could they be friends already? It hadn't even been twenty-four hours yet, and they're over there talking like nothing happened between them. Royal sure was looking good enough to eat standing over there with his shirt off, looking like a tatted up chocolate bar. *Damn.*

I saw Cherry walk out of the club holding Royal's shirt and her purse. She said a few words to Royal, and they both walked towards his car together. He even had the nerve to be holding her by the waist. *Fuck him. Fuck him. Fuck him.* I said to myself.

"I look better anyway." I said trying to contain the anger that was brewing. Kevin finally came back to the car and got in. It took him long enough.

"You good?" he asked.

"I'm forever good." I assured him while going through my purse to find a cigarette. Kevin stared at me for a minute before pulling off.

"I thought you quit smoking." he said after we rode in silence.

"I did, until I ran across a fuck boy." He just nodded his head and didn't say anything else. It was obvious he didn't want to talk about Royal, but shit, I did. I was tired of being sad over him. Every time I see him, it's like I catch even more feelings for him. What kind of shit is that?

"You coming to my house, or am I taking you home?" he asked. That sounded so weird coming from him because I was so used to us living together.

"Take me home." I wanted to drink some more because I felt like I wasn't drunk enough. Well, I was drunk enough. I just wanted to be drunker. I didn't want to think about Royal anymore tonight. I was starting to hate that he always consumed my thoughts. No matter how hard I tried, I just couldn't get him out of my head.

"Who was that light-skinned nigga, and why did y'all look like y'all wanted to kill him?" I asked finishing my cigarette.

"Rome's brother, Raymond." was all he said. I didn't continue to ask questions, because I honestly didn't care.

We finally got to my apartment, and I stumbled up the stairs. Kevin offered to help me, but I didn't want his help. I could do this by myself. I didn't need a nigga for anything, and I never will. I chuckled to myself, because I was really trippin' right now. I unlocked the door and fell right onto the floor.

"Oh shit," I laughed pulling myself up. I was drunk as hell, and I could barely keep my eyes open. I walked to the couch and plopped down on it. Of course, Royal and Cherry popped into my head. I wonder if they were fucking right now, and the thought alone infuriated me. I would kill the both of them. Oh, that sounds like a plan.

I hopped off the couch and went to get my gun. This would be the last nigga to ever break my heart. I wasn't ever going to let another nigga have this hold on me again. He cheated, then tried to act like I was the one in the wrong? Oh no. It doesn't work like that.

I grabbed my car keys and made my way out the apartment. I knew I shouldn't be driving drunk, but right now, I didn't care. I didn't care about anything except getting to Royal's house and showing him not to fuck with me.

I don't even remember how I managed to drive to Royal's house without wrecking, but it was a miracle that I did. I parked right in this nigga's front yard, not even giving a fuck. I laughed as I got out the car.

"Damn, I'm drunk." I said as I stumbled to the door. "Royal!" I yelled banging on the door with my gun. "Open up Royaaaal!" Nobody came to the door, so I kept banging. I knew he heard me, and if he didn't hear me, I was sure his little bitch in there heard me.

"Royal!" I yelled again.

"Kaya, get the fuck on, man!" I heard him yell from the other side of the door.

"Open the fuckin' door, bitch ass nigga!"

"Kaya, I swear to God I'll kill your ass right now if you don't leave!"

I laughed, because he thought that was supposed to scare me. I looked at the doorknob and quickly remembered who the fuck I was. I was the queen of picking locks. Why the hell was I knocking on the door like a basic bitch? Fuck that. I had a gun in my hand, fuck picking the locks.

Shooting the doorknob three times, I kicked the door open and walked in. There was a bitch sitting on the couch watching TV. Damn, this nigga left the club with Cherry, but has a whole different bitch in his house. This nigga really wasn't shit.

"Who the fuck are you?" she asked with a look of disgust on her face. I staggered over to where she was and hit her in the face with my gun until I saw blood. After that, I drug her ass off the couch and out the door. Don't question me, bitch. Don't worry about who I am.

"Oh my gosh!" I heard a voice yell. Turning around, I saw Cherry standing there with a sheet wrapped around her naked body.

"Cherry," I said smiling. "Funny seeing you here, at my nigga's house."

"What? He told me he was single!" she said with her eyes wide with fear.

"He lied to you, bitch!" I charged at her, actually beating her ass this time. That's exactly what she needed. An ass whoopin'. She didn't fight back at all, and it pissed me off. I ended up dragging her out the house too. The only bitch that needs to be in here is me. Royal was nowhere to be found. I guess he went upstairs.

I walked up the stairs so I could look for Royal. I know he heard all the commotion that was going on downstairs. Why didn't he come see what was going on? I know his ass wasn't hiding from little ole me.

"Royal," I sang walking up the stairs. "Come out to plaaaaay."

Walking into his bedroom, I saw him trying to put on his boxers because his nasty ass was naked. I stood at the door and laughed. This was the nigga I was losing my mind over.

"Kaya, what the fuck is your problem, man? How the fuck you keep getting into my house?" he yelled. I ignored everything he was saying as I walked closer to him.

"Don't act like you didn't miss me." I smiled.

"Take your drunk ass on somewhere. I don't miss you." he lied. I could tell he was lying, because he wouldn't look at me.

"Why you lying? Why you acting like I'm some soft ass bitch that won't shoot yo' ass? Why?" He looked at the gun that I had in my hand, then looked at me like I was crazy. The only thing about that was, I was actually crazy.

"Man, you need to chill." I could tell that me holding this gun made him a little nervous.

"Don't tell me to chill, nigga. You put me through all of this shit, when you're the one that cheated! Then you're gonna ignore me like I'm nobody?"

"I called you earlier! You hung up on me!" I rolled my eyes.

"I didn't give a fuck what you had to say. It was irrelevant."

"Then why the fuck you here then?" I swear this nigga was stupid as hell. Why else would I be here? What kinda dumb ass question was that?

"Why do you think I'm here, Royal? I put both the bitches you had in here out. Now you tell me why I'm here."

"What you mean you put them out? You didn't put your hands on them did you?" he had a worried look on his face, like he really cared about these bitches. This nigga was just full of surprises tonight.

"Royal, you know me better than that. Of course I put my hands on them," I laughed. "Well, I put my gun on them. I don't understand why you needed both of them here in the first place! One should've been enough for your nasty ass."

"What the fuck, man. One of those girls was my sister!" He ran past me and down the stairs, and I took off my dress so I could get comfortable. I didn't care that I beat his sister's ass. She was just at the wrong place at the wrong time. Plus, she came at me wrong, so if you ask me, she had it coming. She needs to learn how to talk to people in a polite manner.

After my dress was off, I was going to lay in Royal's bed, but he was probably just fucking Cherry in it, so I decided to go find a guest room. I was pretty sure that he had one in this big ass house.

"Kaya!" I heard Royal calling me, but I ignored him. I was tired as hell now, and all I wanted to do was take my ass to sleep. I would talk to Royal in the morning.

I finally found the guest room, and it looked like a damn master bedroom. It had a bathroom in it and everything. I couldn't help but wonder who the last person to sleep in here was, but at the same time, I didn't really care. I was taking my drunk ass to bed. I collapsed onto the bed and was out like a light without even getting under the covers.

Chapter Fifteen: Royal

"What the fuck, Royal?! Who is that bitch?!" my sister Ava yelled while looking at her beat up face in the mirror.

"That's Kaya… My girlfriend." She turned to look at me with wide eyes.

"Your what?! You had other bitches in here and the whole time you had a girlfriend?! No wonder she came in here and beat my ass! You foul as fuck, Royal. I should tell Mommy on your stupid ass." Ava walked out the bathroom shaking her head and mumbling to herself.

Ava was my half-sister. We had the same mom, but different dads. Her dad was white, while mine was black as hell. She's been living in New York because that's where she wanted to go to school, but she'd just graduated and needed somewhere to live because she didn't want to stay with our mom. I didn't blame her, though. Our mom was always in our business, and the shit was annoying as hell.

"Shit." I muttered to myself walking out the bathroom to go find Kaya. I knew she was crazy, so how she acted tonight didn't even surprise me. She wasn't all the way there in the head. I needed to realize that before she ended up killing my ass like she killed Roxy.

"Look at my face, Royal. That girl beat me with a gun, and I can tell by the look on your face that you're not even surprised that this happened. So tell me, why the fuck aren't you doing right by her?" Ava asked as I tried to walk past her.

"Man... I don't even know. I cheated, she left my ass, I tried to get her back, but she wasn't having that, so I said fuck it. She decided she was ready to talk to me, but I wasn't trying to hear it. She didn't want to talk when I was trying to talk to her ass, so I didn't have shit to say to her."

"Wow. You might be the stupidest nigga on the planet. Go fix shit with her, and pray she doesn't shoot your ass. I hope she beats your ass like she beat mine." Ava continued to shake her head. I sighed and walked back upstairs. Kaya wasn't in my room, and that shocked the hell out of me.

"Kaya!" I yelled, walking out the room and to the guest bedroom that was across the hall. She wasn't in that one either. What the fuck. Why couldn't she just stay her ass in one place? I was not in the mood to be dealing with this shit right now.

I heard loud snoring coming from one of the guest rooms and I walked in it. I should've known she would be in this room. It was the biggest room I had, other than mine. She was laid out on top of the cover in nothing but her underwear. Even when she slept, she still looked sexy as hell. I wasn't sure if I wanted to sleep with her or go back to my room. Shit, I haven't slept with her in a minute, so why not do it now? I got in the bed beside her and pulled her close to my body. I was tired as hell. I would just deal with her in the morning when she's sober.

Waking up the next morning, I was in bed by myself. Damn, she came in here acting all crazy last night just to leave all early the next morning? That's fucked up. I sat up in bed and saw that her phone was still on the dresser, then I heard the toilet flush in the bathroom. She came walking out looking like death.

"Did you wash your hands?" I asked.

"Don't start with me, nigga. It's too early." she mumbled getting back in bed.

"We need to talk about last night." I sighed.

"No, you need to get the fuck out so I can go back to sleep." I smiled at her. She was still rude as hell.

"Nah bae; this my house." She opened her eyes and looked at me.

"I'm not your bae, Royal. Chill with that shit." she chuckled.

"Oh, for real? Then, why you here in my bed then?" I asked with a raised eyebrow. She sat up in the bed and looked around like she didn't know she was in my house.

"How the fuck did I even get here? What happened last night?"

"You got drunk, came over here, beat up my sister and Cherry, waved a gun in my face, then passed out in here." Her mouth fell open, and she shook her head.

"I beat up your sister? Oh my goodness! Is she still here? I need to go apologize!" She got out the bed and tried to leave the room, but I wouldn't let her.

"Chill for right now. She's not even mad about it. She's mad at me." I let her know. She blew out a sigh of relief.

"Good. I don't want her to think I'm a crazy ex-girlfriend that can't let go." I laughed at her.

"Nah, she knows you're my crazy girlfriend." I winked at her.

"Boy, bye. I am not your girlfriend." she said waving me off.

"You are." She looked at me and rolled her eyes.

"Where's my clothes at? Nigga, did you try to fuck last night?" she asked trying to change the subject.

"Nah, don't try to change the subject. You heard what I said."

"I'm not your girlfriend, Royal. You're a cheater, remember?" She laid back down on the bed and closed her eyes. I didn't have anything else to say, so I just kissed her. She didn't push me away like I thought she would, and that only made me wanna fuck.

"Your breath stinks." she said laughing.

"What the hell you think yours smells like? I'm going to get in the shower, you coming?" She smiled at me and pulled me in for another kiss.

"Nope. You just fucked Cherry last night. You're not getting any of my goodies for a long time." She pulled away and turned her back towards me. She got my dick hard just for her to do this bullshit?

"You playing. I bet I hit that shit tomorrow." I said getting off the bed.

"I bet you don't." I walked out of the room so I could go to mine. My phone was ringing on the dresser as soon as I got in there.

"It took you long enough to answer your phone!" Cherry yelled into the phone. I sighed and sat down on the bed.

"What you want, Cherry?" I was not in the mood to deal with her right now.

"You really just let Kaya come in your house and beat my ass like that? You didn't even try to help me! You only helped your sister!"

"Okay. Your point?"

"Why are you treating me like this? You could've at least took me home. I had to call an Uber!" This conversation was pointless. I got what I wanted from her, so there was no need to communicate with her anymore.

"You made it home safe, didn't you?" I asked.

"Yes."

"Then why you callin' my phone bitchin' and shit? What are you getting out of this?"

"You need to handle Kaya. My face is all messed up because of her." Kaya came in here on a rampage last night. She didn't even care. That's my baby though.

"Nah, I don't need to handle shit. You a grown ass woman. It's not my fault you can't fight." I said, nonchalantly.

"She's still at the house with you, isn't she? You're a nasty ass nigga!" I just laughed at her because all of this was funny to me.

"You done?"

"No, I'm not done!" I hung the phone up because I was done with the conversation. She wasn't important to me. She was just some easy pussy and head. That bitch would do anything in the bedroom. She's a hoe, so that's what she gets treated like.

"It doesn't look like you're in the shower to me." Kaya said walking into my room, body looking good as hell. "Oh, there's my dress." She bent down in front of me to pick it up. She knew exactly what she was doing, and it was pissing me off.

"Kaya, get the fuck on before I get you pregnant on purpose." She looked at me with wide eyes before shaking her head.

"Nah. I'm never getting pregnant again. Ain't no babies coming out of this vagina. No sir."

"You not gonna have my babies?" She smiled at me before shaking her head.

"No. I might get me a puppy though."

"So if I wanted to have kids, you wouldn't be with it?" I asked.

"No. First of all, we just started over. You not even getting no ass, so kids should be the furthest thing on your mind." She was really serious about us not having sex. I was almost certain that this wasn't going to last very long. She loved sex more than I did.

"So how long you gonna hold out on a nigga?"

"Well, I was thinking for about a year. Depends on how you act, though." She walked into the bathroom.

"A damn year? Man, hell nah." I said following her. I watched as she turned on the shower and took her underwear off.

"You did this, not me. That's what your punishment is. If you think you can't do it, let me know now so I can be on my way." Her body was looking so damn good, I could barely focus on what she was saying.

"I can do it." I said biting down on my lip. She stepped into the shower smiling at me.

"Now get out. I'm trying to shower." she snapped.

"What? Can I at least watch you since you not giving me none?"

"No, nigga. Get out so I can wash my ass." I shook my head and walked out the bathroom. I decided to go downstairs to get me some orange juice. I doubted Kaya was going to cook me any breakfast. Knowing her fat ass, she probably wanted me to take her to Waffle House or some shit.

"Good morning, brother. I know this is your house and everything, but it would be nice if you would put some clothes on before you came downstairs." Ava said. I forgot that she was even here. I was so used to walking around in nothing but my boxers.

"Oh shit, my bad. I forgot that your ass was even here."

"The door needs to be fixed." she said pointing at the door. I forgot that Kaya's ass had shot the doorknob last night. She was so damn crazy, it didn't make any sense. I sighed to myself.

"I'll get that fixed today." I assured her while I walked into the kitchen. Ava followed me.

"So, did you fix things with her?" Damn, Ava was nosey as hell.

"I guess."

"You're gonna fuck up again. You don't know how to be faithful." I ignored her. I could be faithful. I was just being stupid when I cheated on Kaya. I know not to do that shit ever again, though. "You hear me talking to you. I remember Paisley always calling me and crying over some bullshit that you've done. I'm glad you found you a girl that doesn't take that shit, though. Fuck around and get killed messing with her."

"Why are you in here?" I asked going to the refrigerator.

"Paisley called this morning. She was trying to reach you, but you wouldn't answer your phone. I told her you were upstairs with your girlfriend, and she flipped the fuck out. She started cussing me out like I did something wrong." I stopped what I was doing and turned to look at her.

"You told her I had a girlfriend? The fuck for?!" I yelled. She looked at me with a confused look on her face.

"Why does it matter? You do have a girlfriend, so it doesn't matter what Paisley thinks. She's a damn crackhead anyway. She needs to be picked up at five, though." Ava walked out of the kitchen and went back to sit on the couch. I had forgot about Paisley. There was just too much going on. I knew Kaya would have a problem with me going to pick up my ex, so I wasn't even going to tell her about it.

I didn't know why I cared about what Paisley thought about me having a girlfriend. I didn't even want Paisley anymore like that. Especially, after I walked in on her sucking dick for drugs. That's not the type of woman I need in my life.

"Oh, you poured me some orange juice. You're so sweet." Kaya said walking into the kitchen and taking the cup out of my hand.

"I did not pour that for you." She was wearing a pair of my boxers and one of my shirts. She just made herself comfortable as hell.

"You did. What you got planned today?" She asked like she knew I had to go pick up Paisley later.

"Nothing until five. Why?"

"Damn, nigga. I was just asking a question. I need to go home. I'm not staying here tonight." She took a sip of the orange juice that didn't belong to her.

"What's wrong with my house?" I asked pinching her hard nipple that I could see through her shirt.

"Umm, eww. Ain't no telling how many bitches you've fucked in that bed. I'm not sleeping in that. I don't even want to sleep in that room at all. Roxy's ghost might be trying to haunt me." She started laughing like she had told the funniest joke. It was crazy. You wouldn't be able to tell that Kaya was crazy just by looking at her. I was low-key afraid of her, but I wouldn't let her know that.

"I haven't even had sex with that many bitches in that bed." I lied. She looked at me like she knew I was lying.

"I can tell when you're lying, Royal." She finished off the orange juice and kissed me on my cheek.

"I'm not lying girl." I pulled her close to me and bit her on her neck. That shit almost always made her horny as hell. I felt her body tense up, and she tilted her head back, exposing her neck even more. I had her right where I wanted her… well, I thought I did.

"Royal," she moaned. "You ain't slick, nigga." She pulled away from me and walked out the kitchen. *Damn.* She was really serious about this not having sex shit. I had to get in between her thighs again, and I had to do it soon.

I adjusted my dick in my pants and walked up the stairs to my room so I could take a shower and start my day. I wasn't really looking forward to seeing Paisley later because she was always on some bullshit. I already had it in my head that I wasn't going to say much to her when I picked her up. I've done my job. I got her to quit that drug shit, and now she can be out of my life for good.

"It took you long enough, nigga." Kaya said as soon as I stepped out the shower. She was sitting on the toilet with the lid down, just scrolling through her phone. When the hell did she even get in here? I didn't hear the door open at all.

"You gonna stop sneaking up on a nigga like that." I said while grabbing my towel.

"Ain't nobody sneaking up on you. I wasn't even quiet when I walked in. You just need to be more aware of your surroundings." She shrugged her shoulders as her phone rang. I could tell by the look on her face that she didn't want to talk to whoever was calling.

"Who is that?" I asked.

"Nobody important." She waved me off as she got off the toilet to walk into the bedroom. I felt like she was trying to avoid the question, so I followed right behind her.

"So what's their name?" She turned and looked at me and chuckled.

"Don't turn into one of those niggas. Someone called that I didn't want to talk to, so I ignored it. I haven't asked you who's been blowing up your phone all morning. I could've answered it, but I didn't. Now get off my shit, nigga damn." My eyes immediately went to my phone that was lit up

215

because someone was calling. I already knew it was Paisley, but I wasn't going to answer it with Kaya standing right here. She would know something was up, and I wasn't trying to go through that today. She looked at me with a raised eyebrow as I moved around the room to get dressed. Paisley could wait until I was good and ready to answer the phone. She had already talked to Ava, so why was she still calling me?

"I talked to your sister. I fucked her up pretty bad." Kaya said, pulling me out the thoughts of Paisley.

"Yeah, you did. She was mad as hell about it. Blaming me and shit." I said, shaking my head. I slipped on a pair of boxers and sat down on the bed. Picking up my phone, I silenced it so it would stop ringing. Kaya looked at me with a knowing look, but she didn't say anything about what I had just done.

"It was your fault, but it's all good. I'm over it now." She smiled at me, but I didn't believe shit she was saying.

"If you're over it, then give me some pussy. You playing, man." She rolled her eyes.

"You gotta earn that." was all she said.

"Or I could get it from some other bitch." I tried to say to myself but she heard me anyway.

"We'll go get it from another bitch then, Royal. I'm not going to be here fighting bitches over you anymore. I'll go find me a nigga who knows how to be faithful. It's not that hard." She was still scrolling through her phone like she wasn't bothered by the thought of me cheating on her. She was probably plotting on how she would kill me if I cheated on her again. I didn't say anything else about it. I guess I was going to have to wait however long she wanted me to. This shit was about to be hard as hell.

"I need to be leaving, and I'm hungry as hell." Kaya said standing up.

"Why? What you got planned today?" I asked feeling like she was just rushing to leave so she could talk to whoever called her a few minutes ago.

"Sleep. I'm hungover, my head and stomach hurt, and I just want to sleep. I got way too drunk last night. I'll call you after I wake up." She kissed me on the lips and walked out the room. "Your front door needs to be fixed!" she called up the stairs before I heard the door shut. She's the one who needs to be paying to get my damn door fixed.

I made sure she was gone before I picked up my phone to call Paisley back. I wasn't surprised to see that it started ringing before I could even dail the number.

"Paisley, what the fuck you blowing my phone up for?" I spat as soon as I answered it.

"Because you weren't answering your damn phone! You must've been too busy with your girlfriend since you wanted to ignore me and shit." She was mad at the fact that I had a girlfriend, not that I wasn't answering the phone.

"I was. What that gotta do with you?"

"She's not going to be in the car when you come get me, right?"

"She might be." I said just to fuck with her. Paisley didn't like that at all. She started yelling and cussing my ass out like I wasn't her ride. It was pretty comical to me. "Aight, since you feel that way, find you another ride." I hung up the phone before she could even say anything back. She called right back like I knew she would. I debated on whether I should answer or not. She was really on some other shit right now that I didn't want to deal with. I sighed and decided to answer anyway.

"That was rude, Royal. You didn't have to hang up on me." she said when I answered.

"You trippin' right now, and I ain't with that shit."

"Okay, I'll chill. I just need a ride. I'll be ready at five." she told me like I already didn't know.

"Yeah, aight." I said and ended the call. I didn't know what I saw in that girl when I was dating her. She was annoying as hell. That's probably why we didn't work out. Now that I was thinking about it, I don't even know why I rescued her ass in the first place. I must've really been feeling like Captain Save a Hoe that day. Maybe I cared about her ass more than I thought.

When five o'clock rolled around, I was sitting outside of the building waiting for Paisley's slow ass to come out. I hadn't talked to Kaya since she left my crib earlier, but knowing her, she was probably sleep. That was her favorite thing to do, other than getting money. I planned on showing up at her place as soon as I dropped Paisley off.

I waited for about fifteen more minutes when I finally saw Paisley walking out the building. She was looking like a model. She looked nothing like she did when I dropped her off weeks ago. She was looking better than she did when we were actually a couple. It's crazy how that shit works.

"Hey, sexy." she said while getting in the car. She threw her bags in the back and gave me a hug. "You should let me twist your dreads. Whoever you have doing them now isn't really doing the job right." She ran her fingers through my hair, and I slapped her hand away. She used to twist my dreads for me back when we were together, but that all stopped once we broke up.

"Nah, I'm good." I said driving off. "Where am I dropping you off at?" I asked. I wasn't trying to be around her longer than I needed to be.

"Your house." I looked at her like she was crazy. I thought maybe she might have been joking, but she was serious.

"You already know that's not about to go down."

"But, you said once I got out of rehab, I could stay at your apartment." Damn. I did say that. I wasn't feeling this at all. I didn't want to have to deal with Paisley anymore, and I damn sure didn't want her staying in my apartment, even though I barely used it.

"Stay with your mother." I said, not caring that she probably didn't have anywhere to go.

"No! You want me to get back on drugs, don't you? How do you think I got on them in the first place?" I chuckled.

"Because you're easily influenced."

"Please, Royal. Don't send me back to that house." She said putting her hand on my thigh. I immediately moved her hand and looked at her.

"You gotta problem with keeping your hands to yourself or some shit?" I asked. She just smiled at me. I swear, it was something wrong with this girl.

"Where's your little girlfriend, Royal? I thought you were bringing her with you." She smirked at me, and I just shook my head.

"Don't worry about what my girlfriend is doing. Worry about you not sleeping on the streets."

"Damn, all I did was ask a question. Why are you being so rude to me? What did I ever do to you? You're the one who broke up with me." I ignored her until I pulled up to my apartment. I didn't want her to stay here, but right now, I just needed to get her ass out my car. She was talking too much and asking too many questions. I didn't have time for this shit.

"I'm letting you stay here for now. You have a month to get a job, or I'm putting your ass out, aight?" I asked. She nodded her head and smiled like a little kid on Christmas morning.

"Thank you so much, Royal! You are really the best!" She gave me a kiss on my cheek then got out the car. I gave her the key, she grabbed her bags, then she was on her way. I let out a sigh of relief as she disappeared into the apartment. I should've told her ass to find a different ride. She was always doing too much.

I drove off and headed in the direction of Kaya's apartment. I guess I could've called her first and let her know that I was on the way, but I just wanted to show up. She needed to give me a key so I could just walk in that bitch, but I had a feeling she wouldn't be feeling that shit. She makes everything so difficult.

Pulling into her apartment complex, I saw that nigga Mecca walking up the stairs. I was hoping his bitch ass wasn't about to knock on Kaya's door, and I damn sure hoped Kaya didn't invite him over here. I quickly found a park and jumped out the car. I slowly walked up the stairs because I had to mentally calm myself down. I wouldn't hesitate to kill this nigga right here if he said the wrong thing.

I got to the top of the stairs, and sure enough, that nigga was standing at her door knocking, looking like a sad puppy. I just wanted to know why the hell this bitch ass nigga was here in the first place. This only made me wonder if Kaya was still fucking this nigga. He didn't even notice me standing at the top of the stairs, because he was too damn busy knocking on the door.

Finally, the door swung open, and there stood an angry Kaya looking like she was about ready to body this nigga.

"What the fuck are you doing here, and how the fuck you know where I live at?" she snapped.

"I miss you, and I needed to see your face again." She rolled her eyes and folded her arms.

"That doesn't mean show up at my apartment, nigga. I don't want to see you. I don't want to talk to you. Get the fuck on." She tried to close the door, but he put his foot right there before the door could close.

"Just talk to me. I didn't mean none of the shit I said to you." I chuckled to myself listening to this pathetic ass nigga. It was obvious Kaya didn't want shit to do with this nigga, but he obviously couldn't understand that.

"Bye, nigga!" she yelled still trying to close the door. I decided this should be the time that I step in.

"Nigga, you can't hear or some shit? I know you heard her say bye." I said walking over to him while pulling out the gun I had tucked in my waist. He looked at me with fear in his eyes, but he tried to act like he wasn't afraid at all. I could see right through that shit. He was nothing but a pussy. I realized that when he was at the hospital with Kaya.

"Nah, I can hear." He said.

"Then, why the fuck you still here then? It's obvious she doesn't want to talk to your ass. You can either leave willingly, or you can leave in a body bag. The choice is yours my nigga." He slowly backed away from the door while nodding his head. Bitch ass nigga. Stepping into the apartment, Kaya didn't look too happy to see me either.

"What's up with y'all niggas just popping up at my door without calling first?" She asked, while rubbing the sleep out of her eyes. She was wearing a white shirt, no bra, and a pair of underwear. As always, she was looking good enough to eat. I wanted to take her to the bedroom and tear her ass up.

"I had to pop up to make sure your ass ain't cheating on me." I joked while pulling her in close by the waist. I kissed her on her lips before moving down to her neck. She pushed me off of her and looked at me with her face twisted up.

"Says the one who got caught with a bitch in his bed." She chuckled, but it was more of an annoyed chuckled. "Why you smell like another bitch, Royal?" She asked. My mind immediately went to Paisley. Her ass just had to hug me when she got in the car, and she kissed me on my cheek when she got out. This bitch was really doing too much.

"It's probably Ava. She always sprays a lot of that perfume shit." I quickly lied, and looked away from her. She looked like she didn't want to believe me, so I pulled her in close again.

"You're lying." She said. I hated that she always knew when I was lying. This shit was crazy. Something I will never understand.

"I'm not lying, baby." I kissed her on her neck some more trying to make her forget about what we were talking about.

"Make me kill another bitch, Royal. This time, you're dying with her." She pulled away from me and started walking towards her room. I stood there for a minute and processed what she had just said. I knew she wouldn't hesitate to kill a bitch, but would she actually kill me? She wouldn't do that, right? Shit, she got me feeling a little nervous now. I needed to make sure I stay away from Paisley so Kaya won't think anything is going on between us.

I followed behind her into the bedroom hoping she would stop playing and give up the pussy. She was laying in her bed on her stomach. My dick instantly got hard from looking at her. She knew exactly what she was doing. I pulled her by her leg and made her turn over so that she was on her back.

"Royal," she said giggling. "Go away." I smiled at her and started to remove her underwear. Of course she stopped me, though.

"Kaya, stop playing with me, man." I said as I blew out a frustrated breath.

"I'm not playing. I'm serious about this." I sat down on the bed beside of her.

"This shit isn't even necessary." I complained.

"It wasn't necessary for you to cheat on me either, but you did it anyway. Now you're on punishment. Deal with it." She kissed me on my cheek and laid back down on the bed. She was doing too much with this punishment shit. Me and her not being together should've been punishment enough for me, but no. She had to do it her way. I didn't say anything else to her about it. I just laid back on the bed and closed my eyes. I guess I'll just lay here, hard dick and all.

Chapter Sixteen: Rome

"Babe, answer your phone." Clay groaned. It was late as hell and my phone kept ringing. I was trying to ignore it, and maybe they would get the hint and stop calling, but it didn't work. I groaned picking up the phone and answering it.

"Who is this and why the fuck you calling at two in the morning?" I said into the phone.

"Your voice sounds sexy as hell when you wake up." Tracy said. I sat straight up in the bed and looked over at Clay who, just that fast, was knocked out again. She was snoring and everything. I carefully slid out the bed and made my way downstairs.

"You need to stop with this bullshit, man." I said once I was on the couch.

"You need to come see me. Touching myself to the thought of you isn't working anymore." She must be calling me from a different number because I remember blocking her number after she sent me that nasty ass picture of herself.

"Stop fucking calling me." I snapped.

"I know you want me just as bad as I want you. Clay doesn't have to know. I won't tell if you won't." I could hear it in her voice that she was smiling. That shit didn't do anything but piss me off.

"Leave me alone before I let your daughter know what you're doing." I ended the call before she could say anything else. This was starting to get out of hand. I still hadn't told anyone about what Clay's mom was doing, because I thought she was going to stop, but I was obviously wrong. I didn't want Clay to find out because she would probably accuse me of starting the shit, and I didn't have time for that.

I sighed and leaned my head back against the couch. It seemed like whenever Clay and I got in a good space in our relationship, something was always happening. I looked at my phone to see what time it was, and it was going on three o'clock in the morning. I didn't even want to go back to sleep. I didn't know what to do right now.

Nikki had been calling me nonstop ever since last night. She ended up having to go to the hospital because Kaya's crazy ass busted her shit open with that bottle. I didn't understand why she was calling me like I was going to come to the hospital and visit her ass. The only thing I was trying to do was get rid of her. She had caused way too much drama in my relationship. I was hoping that Kaya had killed her ass last night when she hit her with that bottle. It was like Nikki was one of those bugs that you couldn't get rid of.

"Why are you just sitting down here in the dark by yourself?" I heard Clay's soft voice ask. I turned to see her standing behind me in nothing but my tee shirt. She walked over to me and sat on my lap, then rested her head on my chest.

"I was just thinking about shit." I said sitting my phone down beside me.

"Thinking about what kind of shit?"

"You tryna kill a bitch with me?" Her eyes lit up, and she started smiling hard as hell.

"You don't even know how long I've been waiting for you to ask that." I didn't want Clay doing no crazy shit while she was pregnant, but whenever I tried to kill Nikki, something always went wrong, and it looked bad on my part. I'm tired of that shit. With Clay being with me, she would know that I'm not doing anything I'm not supposed to be doing.

"I'm serious. I don't need you to be all talk, then punk out when it's time to do the shit." She rolled her eyes at me.

"Boy bye, I'll kill that bitch before you even come up with a plan." She flipped her hair, and I put my head down and chuckled.

"Oh, so you're a killer now?" I looked at her with a raised eyebrow.

"No, I'm not a killer, but I could get rid of this Nikki bitch and not lose any sleep over it. I've been waiting to do this since I found out you stuck your dick in that delusional ass bitch." Clay was so confident with what she was saying. I knew she was only talking like this because of Kaya.

"Stop letting Kaya influence you. Killing someone isn't what you think it is. Shit, it could fuck you up in the head just by seeing a dead body." I said. Clay seemed uninterested in what I was saying.

"Kaya doesn't influence me, first of all. I'm pretty sure, if she can kill someone and go on about her life, then I can too. It's not like I'm killing an innocent person. This bitch deserves everything that's coming." She had a point about Nikki deserving this, but I knew once it came down to it, Clay was going to try to back out. I wasn't going to say anything else about it right now. I was going to let her think she was so big and bad, but I knew the truth though.

"You suckin' my dick tonight or nah? You haven't swallowed in a long ass time." I said completely changing the subject.

"I'm not swallowing anymore. You better get used to it." She grinned. I looked at her like she was crazy.

"Fuck you mean you're not swallowing anymore? What kind of shit is that?"

"I'm not swallowing so my baby can eat that! That's her little brothers and sisters! That's nasty, and just wrong." Clay shook her head at me like what she said wasn't weird as hell.

"Man, you know how to ruin a mood." I said laughing.

"We can have sex though."

"Nah, what you just said made my dick soft. I'm good." She shrugged her shoulders and got off my lap.

"Well, I'm going back to bed now. You're welcome to join me if you'd like." I wasn't really tired anymore, but I guess I could lay in bed and watch TV or some shit.

A few hours later, the sun was coming up, and I was up getting ready for work. Clay wasn't in bed with me when I woke up, but that was normal. She was always up before me to make sure I had breakfast before I left. My phone rang as I was putting my shoes on. I didn't want to answer it at first, because I thought it might be Clay's mom on some bullshit again, but I was glad to see it was just that nigga Royal calling.

"Nigga, where the hell you at? What time this shit open?" He said before I could even say anything.

"Fuck you talkin' about?"

"Your shop. What time does your shop open? I see Brandi's stuck up ass in there, but she won't let me in. I'm about to shoot this door down."

"My nigga, if you do that shit, I'm gonna beat yo' ass like Kevin did the other day." Royal started laughing like what I said was funny. I was serious though. Nothing about what I said was a damn joke.

"Nigga, you funny as hell. Just hurry up and bring yo' ass. I need a beer." He hung up on my ass before I could even say anything back. It wasn't even ten o'clock yet, and this nigga was talking about he needed a beer. I got off the bed and made my way downstairs. Clay was standing in the kitchen in nothing but my tee shirt. She turned around and smiled at me.

"Good morning, baby daddy." She threw her arms around my neck and kissed me. She started sucking on my bottom lip making my dick hard instantly. I pulled her closer to my body so she could feel what she was doing to me.

"You feel that? You caused this." I said nibbling on her ear. She started giggling.

"Stop being nasty, Rome." She said trying to walk away from me.

"You started this shit. Let me fuck you on the counter before I have to leave." I tried taking her panties off, but she stopped me.

"No. We both know you don't know how to have a quickie. We're going to be here for another hour, and you're gonna be late for work." She was right, but I wasn't trying hear none of that.

"Man, they'll be aight." I picked her up and carried her into the living room, then sat her down on the couch.

"I'm baking a cake, so you got to be quick." She said unbuckling my pants. Baking a cake? Why was she baking a cake this early in the morning? I'm sure her fat ass is gonna eat all of it by herself and not even save any for me.

"I got you." I lied. This wasn't about to be a quickie. I started kissing her, starting from her tummy, making my way up to her neck, then finally her lips. Clay liked kissing. She would kiss for a whole hour before she even thought about taking her clothes off, and I hated that shit. It wasn't about to go down like that. I positioned myself between her legs, then kissed her again.

"I hope I don't get pregnant." she said with a smile on her face. I didn't say anything back, because I slid into her wetness and couldn't say anything back even if I wanted to.

"Ohhh." she moaned closing her eyes. I pulled all the way out and entered her again. She had me wanting to nut early as hell. It's been like this ever since she got pregnant.

"Shit," I mumbled to myself. I closed my eyes and tried to think of other shit. She wasn't making it any better, because she was grinding into me and moaning loud as hell. I leaned down and bit her on her neck as I sped up. I guess this was going to be a quickie, because I control myself right now.

"I love you, Rome." she moaned while clinging onto me like I was going to leave her. Her eyes were still shut tight, and she was biting down hard on her lip. Her sex faces were making me weaker and weaker.

"Cum for me, baby." I whispered in her ear still trying my hardest to hold out. As soon as I said it, she was cumming all on my dick, and I was right behind her.

"Fuck!" I yelled pulling out of her. She looked at me with a smirk on her face.

"Don't be mad because my pussy is fire." she said sitting up.

"Fuck you." I chuckled and headed upstairs so I could get in the shower again.

"You just did, but you couldn't last." she taunted. I ignored her and continued walking. That didn't go how I planned. I shook my head and got in the shower. Royal was about to be mad as hell because he was going to have to wait a little longer, but he would be alright. If he wanted to drink that bad, he could takc his ass to the damn liquor store. Spend his own money and shit.

After showering again, I sat down with Clay and ate the breakfast she cooked, listened to her talk about some shoes that she wanted me to buy her for our anniversary, kissed her a couple of times, then I was finally on my way. I was an hour late, and the workers were calling, I'm sure to ask where I was at, but I didn't answer. I felt like they were rushing me, and I didn't like to be rushed. I would get there when I got there. They needed to chill with that blowing my phone up shit.

The first thing I noticed when I pulled into the parking lot was Royal. He was leaning up against his car looking mad at the world. I laughed to myself, because he was really out here waiting on my ass like he didn't have shit else to do.

"The fuck took yo' ass so long nigga?" he asked as soon as I got out of the car.

"Clay was looking way too good before I left, so I had to slide up in that real quick." I said walking into the building.

"You ain't even have to tell me that shit." he said with a look of disgust on his face.

"Then your nosey ass shouldn't have asked." He went right over to the mini-fridge and got him a beer out. He looked stressed as hell. I could tell he was high, because his eyes were low as hell.

"Mannnn." he said, plopping down on the couch and blowing out a frustrated breath.

"What's going on with you? Why you over there looking like you got the weight of the world on your shoulders?" I asked.

"Paisley's staying in my apartment."

"What? For what? I thought you took her to rehab."

"I did. She was released and was crying to me about how she didn't have anywhere to go and she didn't want to go back living with her mom because that's the whole reason she started doing drugs in the first place. I wasn't going to let her stay there, but I just needed to get her ass out my car because she was talking too damn much and getting on my nerves."

"You should've took her as back to her mom's crib. Fuck that; she ain't your bitch anymore." I let him know.

"Yeah, I know. Then I get to Kaya's crib, and she's all like 'why you smell like another bitch' and I lied knowing damn well I was with Paisley's ass earlier."

"Wait, you and Kaya good again?" This was news to me. Clay hadn't said anything to me about Kaya and Royal getting back together. She probably didn't know either.

"Yeah. She came to my house straight trippin' the other night. She was drunk as hell for one. She was banging on my door and shit telling me to open it, but I had Cherry upstairs, so I wasn't about to do that. I walk back upstairs and hear a lot of commotion coming from downstairs. Her crazy ass shot my door, pistol whipped Ava and Cherry, then put them both out the house. I didn't even know how to react to that shit. I ain't never dealt with a female that was as crazy as

Kaya. She's on a whole different level of crazy. Shit got me scared, bruh." I couldn't help but laugh. This nigga wasn't afraid of anything, but he was afraid of Kaya?

"You afraid for what?" I asked. He sounded like a pussy right now.

"The fuck you mean? What girl you know kills someone and doesn't lose any sleep over it? That shit ain't normal, bruh. She pistol whipped my damn sister, then threatened my life when I was at her place yesterday." He shook his head like what she said had really bothered him.

"Well, all you gotta do is be faithful this time, and you shouldn't have any more problems. Sound easy to me." I shrugged my shoulders. He started shaking his head even harder.

"She's not giving up the pussy. She told me that I was on punishment, so I have to wait a whole damn year before we can fuck again. A year, my nigga? What type of crazy shit is that? I've never went longer than a damn week, and she's talking about a year? Man, hell nah." I really didn't even have any advice for this nigga. I knew how it felt to lose the woman I loved over a bitch that was just some pussy to me. Clay wasn't as crazy as Kaya though. If she threatened his life, I was pretty sure that she would go through with it. I understood why this would make him afraid of her.

"So what are you gonna do about Paisley?" I asked, changing the subject.

"I don't even know. I gave her a month to get a job and shit, or I'm kicking her out of that apartment, but now I feel like I shouldn't have even done that shit. I just need her out of my life. I know Kaya wouldn't be too happy if she found out I was letting my ex live in my old apartment." He finished off his beer, then got up to get him another one.

"Damn, you better get rid of her before she ends up missing."

"I regret helping her ass out when I saw her that day at the trap house. I should've just minded my damn business and went on about my day." I didn't understand why he was so pressed to help Paisley out in the first damn place. I would've acted like I didn't know who she was when I caught her with a dick in her mouth. I had a feeling that Royal still had feelings for Paisley that he didn't want to admit. That wasn't any of my business though.

"Clay's mom is trying to fuck me." I said, tired of talking about him and his woman problems.

"Man, get the fuck outta here. Her ass hates you; why would she be trying to fuck?" he said laughing.

"The hell if I know. She ran into me at the hospital and told me that Clay can't handle me like she could and bullshit. What kind of shit is that? She acts like Clay isn't her damn daughter. She somehow got my number and was sending me naked pictures and shit, then she called me at like three in the morning today still on that bullshit." I still couldn't believe Clay's mom was acting like this.

"You haven't told Clay, have you?" He finished off his second beer, then lit the blunt that he had sitting behind his ear.

"Hell no. She'll find a way to blame all of this on me. That's some drama that I'm trying to avoid."

"You should've told her as soon as her mom came to you with that bullshit. Clay might've been mad, but now that you've hidden it from her, it makes you look like you're being sneaky." He started nodding his head like he had just told me the best advice ever.

"So, you're gonna tell Kaya about Paisley, right?"

"Man, hell nah. Paisley isn't going to be a problem. All she needs to do is get on her shit, and she won't need me for anything else. Kaya won't even know about her." I didn't say anything back to the stupid shit he just let come out his mouth. I guess he still didn't know that women found out everything. I still didn't understand how they did it. Women be on some straight FBI type shit, and that's why something needs to be done about Clay's mom before Clay found out anything. If I kill Tracy and make it look like it was suicide, Clay wouldn't be too hurt, right?

Chapter Seventeen: Reese

I sat on my couch smiling at the text message that Jay had just sent me. Ever since that day he invited himself into my car, we had been texting each other nonstop. We would talk on the phone at night until I fell asleep too. He was like a breath of fresh air. Even though I didn't want to admit it, I had a little crush on him. I mean, he was gorgeous, and it was a little hard not to have a crush. I wasn't going to let him know that though. His ego was already big enough.

There was a knock on my door, and I was a little afraid to open it. I wasn't expecting any company, and I thought it may have been Kevin showing up to act crazy again, and I didn't want that to happen at all. I really didn't want to see him at all. I just wanted to get over him, then move on with my life.

Getting up from the couch, I quietly made my way to the door. I didn't want whoever it was outside the door to hear me, because, depending on who was on the other side of it, I wasn't going to open it. I looked through the peephole, and I was a little relieved to see Kaya standing outside the door. It was a little weird, because she didn't call before she just showed up. I hated when people did that.

"Kaya? What are you doing here?" I asked once I opened the door. I was hoping Kevin wasn't somewhere lurking in the cut, because I really didn't want to deal with him. Kaya didn't look too pleased to see me. I didn't know why, though. She pushed past me and stepped into my apartment. That's when I noticed that she wasn't alone. The same girl from the club stepped in right behind her and grilled me the whole time. I never met this girl a day in my life, and she's going to come in my apartment acting like this? What in the world?

"We need to talk, Reese." Kaya said with her arms folded. Neither of them sat down. They stood in front of my couch looking at me like I had done something to them. I wasn't understanding this at all.

"About what? Did I miss something? And who is this that you invited to the place I sleep at?" I said, starting to feel some type of way that they were both looking at me like they were ready to fight. I didn't like fighting at all, but I would do it if I had to.

"This is Clay. Rome's girlfriend." Kaya said. She stopped talking so I could let what she said sink in. My eyes grew wide as I looked at Clay. She was still looking at me with the nastiest expression.

"Yep. I'm the girlfriend. I just find it funny how you came to the club with Nikki. All up in the section you knew my nigga was in." I looked at her like she was crazy. Were they really doing this? Were they really in my apartment trying to accuse me of bringing Nikki with me so she could be close to Rome? I didn't even know who Clay was. I damn sure didn't know that I was going to be around Rome that night.

"Are you two really doing this?" I said with a light chuckle.

"Yes we are. Ain't nothing funny about this shit. I suggest you act like you got some sense before you end up like your friend did that night." Clay threatened. I never wanted to hit someone as bad as I wanted to hit her right now. I wanted to hit Kaya, too, because why did she bring this girl to my place? Why didn't she just call me and we talk about this like two civilized adults?

"Look, Kaya invited me to come to the club with her. I told her that I would go and I was bringing a friend, because I didn't want to feel weird and out of place. I didn't know that you were going to be there, and I damn sure didn't know your boyfriend was going to be there. If I would've known that Kevin was going to tag along, then I would've left my behind at home. Nikki wasn't even around me half the night. I don't appreciate you two coming here acting like I've done something wrong, and I didn't even know who Clay was or what she looked like." I folded my arms too because now, I was mad. This was ridiculous! I didn't mess with anyone. I stayed to myself for a reason. To avoid stupid, little girl drama like this.

"I don't believe shit that's coming out of your mouth." Clay said. She had one more chance with me before I hit her in her mouth. Someone needed to do it, and I was feeling like that someone was about to be me.

"Look, I honestly don't care what you believe. I know what the truth is. I haven't even talked to Nikki since that whole thing happened, because she's mad that I was with you two, and she thought I was going to jump in to help her. If y'all wanna be childish and act all mad, then be my guest. I promise I won't lose any sleep over it." Clay was still grilling me while Kaya had a smile on her face. I really didn't understand them. I didn't care anymore. I just wanted the both of them out so I could go back to talking to Jay.

"I've had enough of your smart ass mouth, Reese." Clay snapped, trying to walk closer to me, but Kaya pushed her back.

"Clay, shut your pregnant ass up," Kaya said. "I believe you. You're not the type of person who would do some stupid shit like that. Clay is just mad because she couldn't beat her ass like she wants to because she's pregnant now." I honestly didn't care anymore. I just wanted them out.

"That's nice. Could you see yourselves out, please?" I tried to ask as nicely as possible, but my patience was running thin right now.

"Damn, you don't have to be so rude." Clay mumbled. I ignored her and went to grab my phone and sit down on the couch. They stood there for another minute before they finally realized that I wasn't going to say anything else to them. I was more than happy when they walked out of the door. The first thing I did was call Jay.

"I was wondering what was taking your ass so long to text back, Peanut." he said as soon as he answered.

"Where are you? I need to come over." I said, ignoring what he had just said to me.

"I'm at the crib, why? You miss me or some shit?" I could hear the smile in his voice, and it made me roll my eyes.

"Jay, I'm being serious. I'm about to be over there in like two minutes so put some clothes on." Jay liked walking around his place in nothing but his boxers. It didn't bother me one bit, but it made it hard for me to focus.

"Alright." he said laughing. I ended the call and quickly put my favorite bedroom shoes on. They were black and had white bunnies all over them. I thought they were the cutest things, so I just had to buy them. Before leaving out the door, I went to the bathroom to make sure I looked good. I found myself doing this a lot lately. I had to make sure I looked nice before Jay saw me.

Once I was satisfied with my appearance, I walked out the door and down the hall to his apartment. I didn't understand why this man had me feeling so nervous all the time, but he did. My hands were sweating, and my mouth got dry instantly. This always happens, and I was really growing tired of it. I knocked on his door and waited patiently for him to come open it.

He opened the door in nothing but his boxers. Blunt hanging from his mouth, a bottle of Hennessy in one of his hands, and he wore that dorky smile on his face, that he always does when he sees me now. I rolled my eyes and stepped into the apartment.

"Jay, I told you to put some clothes on." I said sitting down on the couch. He finally had furniture in his apartment, and it actually looked like someone lived here.

"Yeah, I heard you when you said that stupid shit," he said, sitting down right beside me on the couch. "Why would I put on clothes when I'm chillin' in my place? I'm comfortable as fuck right now." I rolled my eyes at him. All I wanted to do was talk, and he wanted to be damn near naked, looking like a sexy Greek god.

"Whatever, Jay." I said waving him off. "Guess what just happened to me?"

"What happened to you? Is it something serious? You be being dramatic as fuck sometimes." I ignored his last statement and proceeded to tell him what had just happened with Kaya and Clay. When I was finished, he didn't say anything; he just handed me the blunt that he had. I looked at it like it was the scum of the earth.

"What are you handing me that for? I don't smoke, Jay." I said.

"Yeah, I know, but maybe you should start." He shrugged his shoulders, but I didn't take it. I was still just looking at it like it was the worst thing ever. I'd never smoked a day before in my life. I've always been a drinker, but never a smoker. It just didn't seem fun to me. "Take it. I'll tell you how to do it." he said, after he saw that I was just going to stare at it. Reluctantly, I took the blunt out of his hand and slowly raised it to my mouth.

"Now what?" I asked.

"Smoke that shit. Don't get it wet though." I inhaled and blew the smoke right back out. By the look on his face, I could tell that I was doing something wrong.

"You wasting it! Inhale it, Peanut. Don't blow anything out." I sighed, but did as he said. I wasn't prepared for what happened next. I basically tried to swallow the smoke, if that even makes sense, then I start coughing uncontrollably. My chest started burning, and my eyes started watering up.

"There you go," he said laughing. "You did it right; you just got baby lungs." I did it right? Then, why the hell did I feel like this? Why did I feel like I was about to cough up a lung? He didn't cough at all when he smoked. I was embarrassed, so I just passed the blunt back to him.

"Here." I said through my coughs.

"Nah," he shook his head. "Do it again." I looked at him like he was crazy.

"What? No, my chest hurts too bad. Go get me some water or something."

"Do it again, Reese." I blew out a frustrated breath, but I did it all over again. I got the same result, and I really wasn't feeling this anymore. I needed something to drink because my chest felt like it was on fire.

About ten minutes later, I felt like I was floating. I was laughing at everything, and it felt like everything was happening in slow motion. I looked at Jay through my low eyes and smiled at him. For this first time since I met him, he didn't have his hair up in a man bun. It was down, and it came a little past his shoulders. He was looking better than he usually did.

"Stop staring at me like that." he said looking at me with those low blue eyes. I just started laughing. I honestly didn't even know what it was that I was laughing at, and eventually, he started laughing with me.

"Clay," I scoffed once we finished laughing together. "What kinda name is that anyway? The girl is named after mud."

"And you're named after candy." He licked his lips.

"Shut up. I'm trying to be serious."

"What's the deal with you and your ex?" The question caught me off guard. I didn't want to talk about Kevin. The whole reason I wanted to be around Jay in the first place was so I wouldn't think about Kevin at all.

"What do you mean?"

"What happened between you two? He seems to still be crazy about you. I mean, I don't blame him. I'd be crazy over yo' sexy chocolate ass too." I chuckled and pushed him playfully.

"There's not much to say about that. He cheated, I broke up with him, now he wants me back." I rolled my eyes just thinking about it. The whole situation still made me upset.

"Damn. Sucks for him. That's why he was so mad when he came to your crib that night. He thought we were together or some shit."

"Yeah. I don't understand that though. He cheated on me with another woman, but as soon as he thinks I'm moving on, he's ready to kill everyone. It just doesn't make sense." I shook my head.

"That's a man for you. We all do that shit." he shrugged his shoulders.

"So if we were together, you would cheat on me, then get mad when you saw me with another dude?" I asked. I start wondering what it would be like to be in a relationship with him.

"I can't even answer that question for you, Peanut. Men don't get in relationships with it already in their mind that they're going to cheat. It happens unexpectedly." I didn't want to hear any of this right now. I didn't want to talk about Kevin. I just wanted to be over him.

"What's your real name?" I asked, changing the subject. He looked at me like he didn't want to answer the question.

"Jay is my name." he said.

"No, that's what you want everyone to call you. I want to know what name was given to you at birth." He sighed, like it was so hard to tell me what his name was.

"Jason." Really? He acted like he had a weird or ghetto name or something. It was regular. He didn't look like his name would be Jason at all.

"That's cute." I beamed. He shook his head at me.

"Stop that shit."

"Why don't you like it? It's not even bad."

"I got a twin brother named Mason. He was the fuckin' angel child in everyone's eyes for some reason. My parents treated his ass like royalty, but treated me like shit, because I stayed in trouble. I don't like my brother, and the feeling is mutual. So, I'd rather be called Jay because our names rhyme and I'm trying my hardest to forget about that family all together." I didn't even know that Jay had a twin. I wondered what he looked like. Did he have tattoos too? Could he put his hair up in a man bun? Did he look like delicious white chocolate like Jay did?

"I wanna meet him." I said aloud. I meant to say it in my head, but it came out. Jay looked at me like I was crazy.

"The fuck for?" I couldn't help but smile at his aggressiveness that just came out of nowhere. Something about that turned me on, when I knew it shouldn't have.

"Because I just do. I want to meet all of your family. See what they're like." He shook his head vigorously.

"No. Hell no. Fuck them. Fuck every single one of them." He was so passionate with his words, but I still wanted to meet them.

"That's not very nice." He ignored me, so I start running my fingers through his hair. I couldn't help but wonder what his body would feel like on top of mine, or what his lips would feel like on mine again. It was like he knew what I was thinking, because he pulled me closer to him and put his lips on mine.

It was everything I expected it to be. His lips felt just like I imagined they would. He tasted like the alcohol he was drinking and the blunt he was smoking, but I'm pretty sure my breath wasn't too fresh either. He quickly pulled away and looked at me like he didn't mean to kiss me.

"Damn… My bad. I ain't even mean to do that." He said looking nervous. He was acting like we had never kissed or something.

"Can you do it again?" I guess that's all he wanted to hear, because he came back in, but this time it was more forceful. He slid one hand up my shirt and played with one of my breasts, while the other one fumbled with my pants. I wanted to tell him to stop, but the way he was making me feel while playing with my nipple had me wanting it to take all my clothes off. I let out a small moan once I felt his fingers slip inside of my wetness.

"Shit, Reese." He said against my mouth. I needed to stop him, but I couldn't. Everything he was doing was making me weaker and weaker. He gently laid me back on the couch while still kissing me. That's when Kevin's face popped up in my head.

"Stop," I said pushing him off of me. "I can't do this." I quickly fixed my pants and pulled my shirt down. I was up and out the door before he could even say anything to me.

"Reese!" I heard him yell, but I continued to my apartment. I already knew that sex with Jay would be everything and more, but I just couldn't even bring myself to do it. I wasn't over Kevin at all, and it wouldn't be right to have sex with Jay.

I couldn't help but smile at how Jay had my body feeling. If only he would've come in my life at a different time, things between us would be so different, but I guess everything happens for a reason, and Jay and I would have to stay strictly friends. Nothing less, and nothing more.

Chapter Eighteen: Royal

"How the fuck you get my number, Paisley?" I said sighing into the phone. She had been blowing me up all day, and I finally decided to answer. She was calling from an unknown number, and if I would've known it was her, I would've never answered.

"I have my ways." I could hear the smile in her voice, and that made me want to wring her neck.

"What you want? I'm at my girl's crib, and she wouldn't be happy if she knew you were blowing my phone up." She smacked her lips.

"I don't care about her. It's been three weeks since you dropped me off here, and you haven't even been by to see me. I'm bored, lonely, and I miss you. I'm pretty sure your girlfriend wouldn't mind if you came to visit an old friend." Paisley obviously didn't know who Kaya was and what she was about.

"Nah, she would mind, and you would probably end up dead somewhere in a ditch. Stop calling me, Paisley." I said getting ready to end the call.

"Wait! Can you please just take me to my mom's place? That's all I need from you." I sighed again. I didn't want to be around her at all. I just wanted to forget I ever met her and go on with my life, but she obviously didn't want that to happen though.

"Aight, man. I'll be over there tomorrow or some shit." I let her know then hung up before she could even say anything else. I was just going to tell her that she needed to get her shit out that apartment and go. She was trying to get me in trouble with Kaya, and I didn't need that right now.

I got out of my car and made my way to Kaya's apartment. She wasn't expecting me, because I didn't call, but I never called anymore. I just showed up because I could.

I checked to see if the door was unlocked, and to my surprise, it actually was. Kaya always kept her door locked, because she was paranoid as hell. I stepped in and was hit in the face with the smell of brownies. Them shits were smelling good as hell, too. Kaya was standing at the stove in nothing but her underwear, singing to herself. I quietly shut the door behind me and snuck up behind her.

"Hey, sexy." I said. She jumped, turned around, and had a gun aimed at my head all in like two seconds. I wasn't expecting this, but then again, everything was unexpected when it came to her.

"Oh, it's just you," she said with a sigh of relief. "I thought you were an unwanted guest or something. This is why I never keep my door unlocked." I shook my head at her.

"Kaya, you got fuckin' problems, man."

"No I don't. I'd rather be safe than sorry." She shrugged her shoulders.

"But that shit turned a nigga on though." I said biting my bottom lip. She smirked at me and slowly licked her brownie. She was staring into my eyes the whole time she did it too. She was really trying me right now. She was already looking extra good in her white lace bra and underwear. I could see her nipples through the thin fabric, and she had a thong on not really covering anything. I was hard as hell, and this no sex thing wasn't about to work.

I grabbed her by the waist and pulled her closer to me. Before she could even protest, I was tonguing her down and trying to remove her underwear. She slapped my hand away and backed away from me.

"Royal, we're not having sex." she said while folding her arms.

"Yes we are." I picked her up and threw her over my shoulder.

"Royal! Put me down! Nigga, I swear to God if you drop me, I'm killing your stupid ass!" she yelled. I ignored her as I walked into her bedroom and threw her on the bed. She liked that rough shit, and that's exactly what I was about to give her. I snatched her thong off and brought it up to my nose, sniffing it hard as hell before putting it in my back pocket. She sat on the bed with her arms folded, pouting like the big ass baby she was.

"Fix ya face, beautiful." I said smirking at her. She rolled her eyes, and I laid her back on the bed. She didn't have a problem opening her legs. She knew she wanted this just as bad as I did. I dove right in making her moan out in pleasure. She was arching her back and running her hands through my dreads.

"Royal," she moaned, while looking down at me. She was beautiful as fuck. "Ohh shit." Her body start shaking as she came all in my mouth. It hadn't even been a full five minutes, and she was already cumming. I smiled to myself as I stood up and removed my clothing. She was laying on the bed still trying to catch her breath with her eyes closed.

Positioning myself between her legs, I looked directly in her low eyes, then started kissing her on her neck.

"You sure you don't want me to do this?" I asked. She nodded her head and I slowly entered her. "Shit." I had to just sit there for a minute, because I didn't want to nut too quick.

"Stop playing with me, nigga. You wanted it, now fuck me." she demanded.

"Shut the fuck up, Kaya." I slowly started moving in and out of her, and she held on to me like she never wanted me to leave her. She held out for two weeks. I didn't think she was going to last that long, but her crazy ass did. I didn't even think I could do it. There were so many bitches that I could've just called up, but I didn't because I actually wanted to make things work with Kaya. I also didn't need her trying to kill anyone else because of some stupid shit that I did.

She bit her lip as she tried to contain her moans, but that shit wasn't working. Her eyes were rolling to the back of her head, and she was digging her nails into my arms. I was too focused on how she was feeling to let her know that her nails were hurting like shit. I didn't want to sound like a little bitch either.

Kaya pushed me off of her, then made me lay down. I wanted to be in control the whole time, but I should've known that Kaya wasn't going to have that. She got on top and smiled at me.

"You think you're gonna be able to handle this?" she asked.

"I know I can." The look on her face let me know that she was going to do some crazy shit. I could keep up, though. She wasn't about to out fuck me.

She started off by slowly grinding on me, while trying to unsnap her bra. I had to close my eyes, because the faces she was making, and the way her titties were bouncing all in my face was enough to make me bust right here, right now.

"Shit." I said to myself, grabbing her hips to try to get her to slow down a little bit. That didn't do anything but make her speed up. She had me moaning out like a little bitch, and my toes were curling.

"I thought you could keep up, Royal." she said through her moans.

"I am." I lied. She laughed and leaned down to kiss me.

"You're not even looking at me, baby. Open your eyes." I slowly opened my eyes and looked at her. She was enjoying seeing me like this. I could see it all in her face that she was on the verge of cumming, I grabbed her hips and thrust upward. She screamed out, and I felt her muscles tighten around me. She came hard as hell, and I was right behind her. She fell over on the bed and closed her eyes.

"You're still on punishment." she said trying to catch her breath.

"Man, I ain't trying to hear that shit, Kaya. Two weeks was long enough. I expect to get that pussy every night." I was serious as hell. She had me fucked up if she thought she was going to hold out on me again.

"Nigga, stop showing up at my place without calling first. That shit's annoying as hell."

"That's another thing; you staying here isn't about to work anymore." She turned to look at me. She was ready to argue, I could see it all over her face.

"What? I'm paying for this apartment, so I'm going to live in this apartment. Fuck you mean?"

"You're moving in with me. That's what I mean. I don't care about all that extra shit you're talking about right now."

"I don't want to live in that house, Royal. I don't even want to be in it for longer than five minutes. I'm staying at my apartment, and that's the end of it." I laughed, because she thought she was running some shit.

"I'll buy another house then. Will that make you feel better?" She smiled at me.

"Yes. I want a big ass house, too. It has to be bigger than the one you have right now." I just looked at her. It wasn't like I couldn't afford that shit. I just didn't want a house bigger than the one I had now. What was the point if no one was going to be living there but me and Kaya?

"Nah," I said sitting up in the bed. "It might be the same size, maybe even smaller. I'm not getting a big ass house only for us two to live in. That shit is stupid." The look on her face let me know that she wasn't feeling what I had just told her, but I really didn't care.

"I don't understand why you just can't move in with me anyway." she said with an eye roll.

"I don't want to live in this small ass apartment, Kaya. That shit ain't gonna work." she waved me off.

"Whatever, nigga. Do what you gotta do." She got off the bed and walked into the kitchen. I followed right behind her.

"You're not mad at me, are you?" I asked, hugging her from behind.

"No, I'm hungry. I'm about to eat this whole plate of brownies." She smiled to herself and picked up the plate. "Find a movie to watch." she said, while walking into the living room to sit on the couch. We both didn't have any clothes on, and she was just chillin' like this shit was normal for her. Knowing Kaya, she probably did walk around the house naked. That seems like some shit she would do.

"You find a movie to watch. This is your crib, not mine." She looked up at me, while stuffing her face with a brownie.

"Our crib." She smiled. I sat down on the couch beside her. I reached for a brownie, and she slapped my hand away. "Do you want a brownie?" she asked. What kinda stupid ass question was that? I obviously reached for a brownie because I wanted one.

"Yeah, man."

"Well, I guess you better go make you some then because you ain't getting any of mine." She picked up the remote and turned the TV on. She was such a fat ass.

"That's fucked up. You really not gonna give your man a brownie?" She looked at me and smacked her lips.

"Here man! You always begging for my food." She handed me the plate of brownies, then found a movie for us to watch. Of course her childish ass found a cartoon movie to watch, and she knew all the words to it. I didn't even know what the movie was called. The shit was stupid, though.

Once the movie was over, I decided that I would go take Paisley to her mom's place so she wouldn't start calling and blowing my phone up.

"Where are you going?" Kaya asked as she followed me into the bedroom and watched me put my clothes back on.

"I gotta go handle some shit. I'll be back later, though." I kissed her on her forehead and made my way out the apartment. I was shocked that Kaya didn't question me more about where I was going, but I was glad she didn't. I couldn't think of a lie to tell her, and she probably would've known that I was lying anyway.

I got in my car and let out a loud sigh. I didn't want to deal with Paisley and her shit today. I already knew that she was about to be on some other shit, and I didn't have time for this. I just wanted to drop her ass off and keep it moving. As I was driving, I dialed her number.

"It took you long enough. Are you finally finished with your girlfriend?" She asked with an attitude.

"Yo, chill with that shit. Be glad that I'm even taking yo' ass somewhere. I could've stayed my ass at my girl's crib and been dicking her down for the rest of the day, and not dealing with your ass."

"You just had to throw your little girlfriend in my face. I don't want to hear about her." I chuckled lightly.

"And I don't want to drive you to your mom's, but I'm doing it anyway. You can always get what you want in life." I let her know.

"Whatever, Royal."

"I'll be there in like ten minutes, so be outside." I said, then hung up. I didn't even care if she was finished talking or not. She would get over it.

Paisley was outside waiting for me like I told her to be. I was shocked that she even listened. Her eyes lit up when she saw me, and she quickly made her way to the car.

"I swear, you look better and better each time I see you." She smiled.

"Where ya moms live at?" I asked, ignoring what she just said to me. There was no need for her to tell me how I looked. There was no need for her to talk to me at all.

"You know you remember where my mom lives. Stop playing." She laughed. I didn't say anything else to her. I just turned up the music so she would get the hint that I didn't want to talk to her ass. She didn't though. She turned the music right down and started talking again. "What's your girlfriend's name?" I glanced over at her.

"Why?" I knew she was up to something. She was always up to something.

"Because, I just want to know."

"None of your damn business." She rolled her eyes.

"Whatever. You're being real extra right now."

"And you're being real annoying right now. Why can't you just be quiet?" That was all I wanted from her. If she would stop talking, this car ride would be so much better.

"Because I don't want to. Oh yeah! I meant to tell you that I saw some nigga the other day with that same chain you had once. You know, the gold one, with the letter R on it?" I looked over at her again.

"Who was it?" I asked. I knew for a fact that chain was mine, because someone had stolen it out my crib a while ago.

"I don't know. Some nigga that lives in the apartment complex. It looked just like yours." Now, my blood was boiling. First, the nigga robs me for it, then he's out rocking that shit like it's his?

"Man, that shit probably was mine. Someone stole it out my house." She looked shocked after I told her that.

"Really? Who was it?"

"The hell if I know, but once I find out, it's over for that nigga." I said more to myself.

"Don't you have cameras in your house? Why didn't you check them?" I felt stupid as hell. I had cameras all over my house, and I didn't think about them at all once I got robbed. I probably could've been found out who did this shit. I didn't even say anything back to Paisley. I was consumed with my own thoughts right now. I needed to hurry up and drop her ass off so I could go to my crib and look at the tapes.

Paisley couldn't get out the car fast enough when I pulled up to her mom's crib. Her mom was sitting on the porch looking like a straight crackhead. She smiled and waved, but I ignored her as I backed out of the driveway. I didn't mean to be rude, but my thoughts were everywhere right now.

I think I broke every traffic law to get to my place. Kaya called me, but I sent her straight to voicemail. I would call her back after I was finished trying to figure out who it was that robbed me. She called back two more times, but I still didn't answer. I hoped whatever it was that she was calling about wasn't that serious.

"Well hey, Royal!" Ava called as I basically ran past her to go upstairs. She was sitting on the couch watching TV, like she always was. I didn't have time to speak to her right now. We could talk after I was finished.

Once I pulled up the videos on my computer, I went back to the day I was robbed. I could see two people walk in through the back door. One was a female, and the other was a nigga. How the hell did they get in so easily? I really needed to get an alarm system or some shit.

I was shocked to see that a female actually robbed me. It was obvious that the woman knew what she was doing, because she had on a ski mask, while the dude didn't. He was looking like he was scared to even be in the house.

There was something very familiar about the girl though. Her body looked really familiar. She turned to the side, and I was in for the shock of my life. I knew only one person with that tattoo that took up her whole right arm. It was dark, but I could still see that shit. Mad was an understatement. I was fuming. I got up and stormed out the house. Now it was my turn to act crazy.

Chapter Nineteen: Kaya

"So your bitch ass boyfriend was supposed to scare me or some shit?" Mecca asked over the phone. I rolled my eyes. Why did I even answer the phone for this stupid ass nigga? I should've just sent his ass to voicemail like I'd been doing.

"Nigga, stop playing. You were scared. I saw the face you made when he pulled that gun out. Fuck outta here." I laughed.

"Ain't nobody scared of that nigga."

"Did you really call me just to talk about my boyfriend? That's some straight bitch shit, Mecca."

"Yo' chill with that shit. I called because I wanted to talk to you." I sighed. I already knew where this conversation was going. I should just hang up right now.

"Talk about what, Mecca?"

"Us." I laughed to myself.

"Us? There ain't no us anymore. I'm happy and in a relationship. You're with Erica, so be with her. Stop calling me and trying to fuck. I'm not fucking with you no more. Get that through your head." I ended the call before he could even say anything back. Mecca was starting to become a problem for me. I decided to call Royal to let him know about Mecca, but his ass sent me right to voicemail. *Hmm, let me try this again because maybe it was an accident.* I got the same result as

I called back two more times, and I started to feel some type of way.

Why wasn't he answering the phone? What was he doing that was so important that he couldn't answer the phone for me? Maybe his phone was dead. Yeah, that's exactly what it was, because he wouldn't ignore me now that we were back together, right? Right.

I wanted to call Clay and see what she was doing today, but I decided against it. I would just chill by myself until Royal got back. Shit, he better bring his ass back and let me know why the fuck he wasn't answering his damn phone.

I walked into my bedroom and laid out on the bed. Since I was bored, there was nothing better to do but take a nap. I put on an oversized tee shirt with nothing on underneath and got under the covers. This nap was about to be lovely. They always were.

    ***

When I woke back up, it was dark outside. I had really slept for the whole day. I was really tired because Royal had given me some of the best dick of my life, earlier. That nigga was something serious when it came to sex. I swear, his sex should be illegal because it will make any bitch crazy.

I sat up in bed, and I was shocked to see Royal just standing there looking like a damn creep. It was dark, but I could still see his ass.

"Royal, what the fuck? Why you just standing there in the dark and shit?" He didn't say anything. He just walked to turn the light on, then walked closer to me. He pulled his gun out and pressed it against my head.

"You really thought you were gonna rob me and I wasn't going to find out?" He looked at me with nothing but murder in his eyes. I smiled at him.

"Shoot me, nigga."

To Be Continued…

CPSIA information can be obtained
at www.ICGtesting.com
Printed in the USA
LVOW10s0037280217
525566LV00016B/205/P

9 781542 324748